At Heart

At Heart

NEWFOUNDLAND SHORT STORIES

Lisa Ivany

and

Robert Hunt

FLANKER PRESS LTD.
ST. JOHN'S, NL

Library and Archives Canada Cataloguing in Publication

Ivany, Lisa J., 1965-
  At heart : short stories / Lisa Ivany and Robert Hunt.

ISBN 1-894463-95-1

  I. Hunt, Robert J., 1949- II. Title.

PS8617.V36A84 2006   C813'.6   C2006-905209-3

© 2006 by Lisa Ivany and Robert Hunt

ALL RIGHTS RESERVED. No part of the work covered by the copyright hereon may be reproduced or used in any form or by any means—graphic, electronic or mechanical—without the written permission of the publisher. Any request for photocopying, recording, taping or information storage and retrieval systems of any part of this book shall be directed to Access Copyright, The Canadian Copyright Licensing Agency, 1 Yonge Street, Suite 800, Toronto, ON M5E 1E5. This applies to classroom use as well.

PRINTED IN CANADA

FLANKER PRESS
ST. JOHN'S, NL, CANADA
TOLL FREE: 1-866-739-4420
WWW.FLANKERPRESS.COM

First Canadian edition printed October 2006

10 9 8 7 6 5 4 3 2 1

We acknowledge the financial support of: the Government of Canada through the Book Publishing Industry Development Program (BPIDP); the Canada Council for the Arts which last year invested $20.0 million in writing and publishing throughout Canada; the Government of Newfoundland and Labrador, Department of Tourism, Culture and Recreation.

CONTENTS

1. WHISPER 1
   by Lisa Ivany and Robert Hunt

2. SUNSET HILL 10
   by Lisa Ivany

3. DANNY WONDER 36
   by Robert Hunt

4. STANDOFF AT WIDOW'S PEAK 46
   by Lisa Ivany

5. STEEL MOUNTAIN 66
   by Robert Hunt

6. LUCKY'S LANDING 72
   by Lisa Ivany

7. SNIPER 86
   by Robert Hunt

8. EVER AFTER 94
   by Lisa Ivany

9. FOUR DAYS IN JULY 103
   by Robert Hunt

10. MOON RIDER 113
    by Lisa Ivany and Robert Hunt

11. INTERN WITH A SECRET 127
    by Lisa Ivany

12. CROSSING THE TUBE 143
    by Robert Hunt

13. SILENCING THE DEMONS 152
    by Lisa Ivany

14. STAY WITH ME 161
    by Robert Hunt

15. STRANGER BEHIND THE MASK 169
    by Lisa Ivany

16. RECONCILIATION 177
    by Robert Hunt

17. RENDEZVOUS WITH DESTINY 188
    by Lisa Ivany

18. ANGELA'S WINGS 196
    by Robert Hunt

Acknowledgements

This book contains stories of fiction, some inspired by true events. Where necessary, names of people and places have been changed to protect the identities of those involved.

To my family, especially my wonderful mother, Maggie Ivany, who is the centre of my universe. Also in memory of Ben Ivany, who passed away before seeing his daughter's name in print.

Lisa Ivany

To Sharon and my two children, Stephen and Heather, for their support.

Robert Hunt

Whisper

LISA IVANY and ROBERT HUNT

His name was Whisper and he moved like the wind. He was the favoured horse to win today at the Toronto racetrack and was sure to give a good performance. His satin coat was dark brown except for one perfectly shaped white crescent centred just above his eyes. His coat glistened with heavy sweat and steam as he turned the final corner, heading for the finish line.

A light snowfall covered the course on this chilly February day as he rounded the oval track toward certain victory. Brody's Boy was parallel to him, but Whisper increased his lead as the horses edged closer to their goal. He bypassed the last corner rail as if the others were in slow motion.

Whisper's jockey, Lester Barnett, knew victory was

theirs for the taking. They moved along the inside rail, just half a furlong ahead of Brody's Boy and a full length in front of Princess, who was running third. The jockey leaned forward in the saddle. His black-visored cap pinned his blond hair in place, enabling his sea-blue eyes an unobstructed view.

Then it happened. Brody's Boy, on the outside, crowded Whisper, pushing him toward the railing. Whisper and Lester were hugging the rail, and Lester knew they were in serious trouble. The sound of crunching bone split the air as Whisper crashed against the rail, followed by a loud snap as his leg gave way beneath him. Several riders, who were luckily three lengths behind, avoided the spill and veered away from the carnage.

Lester was unsaddled, and while Whisper went down in a heap on the track, his rider flew across the rail. Over and over Lester tumbled, finally stopping on the grass twenty feet inside the track. Both rider and horse lay unconscious as onlookers stared in horror.

Lester awoke the next morning in Mount Sinai Hospital, just a short distance from the racetrack. Several ribs had been bruised and his left leg sprained from the impact with the rail. Meanwhile, when Whisper was examined by the racetrack's staff veterinarian, it was determined that Whisper had a fractured leg. Sam Davis was the horse's owner. He knew Whisper would never run again, so he decided to have him put to sleep. When this news reached

AT HEART

Lester, he immediately hopped out of bed and limped to the nursing station.

"Nurse, I have to be discharged right away!" he exclaimed.

"Mr. Barnett, you're in no condition to leave the hospital."

"It's an emergency! I have to leave now!"

"You'll have to wait until morning, when your doctor comes on duty. He's the only one who has the authority to release you," the nurse replied.

Lester returned to his room and paced the floor in frustration. He had to leave, even if it was against medical advice. He quickly slipped into his clothes and crept down the hallway, in the opposite direction of the nursing station, and entered the elevator undetected.

He arrived at the racetrack seconds before Whisper's demise. The vet had filled the syringe and was ready to inject when Lester burst in upon him.

"Wait!" Lester yelled.

The doctor and Sam Davis both looked up.

"What are you doing out of the hospital?" Sam asked.

"I heard about your plan for Whisper and I had to stop it."

"I know you've become attached to the horse, but he will never be able to race again," Sam explained. "Who will want a racehorse that can't race?"

"My daughter will," Lester replied. He thought of the

joy on Kristy's face when he returned home with the horse she had always loved. They would arrive just in time for her eleventh birthday.

"He's all yours, then," Sam responded. "I'm sure he's in good hands with Kristy."

The trip home took longer than expected, as Lester had to make numerous stops to tend to Whisper's injuries. The stallion lay upon the hay in the U-haul for the entirety of the trip, and Lester wondered if the horse would recover, or succumb to its injuries.

Two weeks after the accident, Lester pulled into the driveway of his home in Norris Point. He was glad to see the lane had been plowed, right up to the stable in the east field.

Crouched upon the snow in the open field, Kristy wasn't aware of her father's arrival as she rolled a ball of snow to the right size for her snowman's head. Her tiny round face and rosy cheeks peeked out from the pink hood of her snowsuit. She was bundled well for the weather, with only a few stray wisps of blond hair escaping her hood. As she stood on tiptoes to place a carrot on the snowman's face, she heard a car door slam shut and looked to see her father. She bounded over the field as fast as her legs would take her.

"Daddy, you're home!" she squealed with delight.

"Hi, sweetheart," Lester replied and swept her into his arms for a warm kiss. "Happy birthday."

AT HEART

"It was yesterday," Kristy said.

"I'm sorry I missed it, honey, but I got here as fast as I could. We can still celebrate it today, can't we?"

"Okay, Daddy. So, where's my present?"

Lester laughed and opened the door to the U-haul. "Right here," he said.

Amazingly, Whisper was on his feet and moving his head to sniff the cold winter air of Newfoundland for the first time. Gingerly, he walked down the ramp with only a slight limp in evidence.

"It's Whisper!" Kristy shrieked. "Is he really mine?"

"As long as you take care of him, you can keep him."

"Oh I will, Daddy. I will!"

Kristy was true to her word and faithfully nursed Whisper back to health. She took on the sole responsibility of feeding, grooming, and exercising the fine stallion. She even performed the not-so-glamorous chore of cleaning his stall. The bond between Whisper and Kristy grew stronger with each passing day, and he would nuzzle her face upon receipt of the apples she would have tucked in her pockets. As February crept into March, Whisper's strength gradually returned. The fracture had mended, but had left his injured leg slightly weaker than the others.

By mid-March, the residents of Norris Point were enjoying an unseasonably warm temperature. The snow had almost melted completely, to the point where Kristy saddled up Whisper and took him for daily trots around the fields near her home. The horse's previous breakneck speed was only a memory, but it suited Kristy just fine.

"Daddy," Kristy yelled from atop Whisper one morning. "Come and ride with us."

"Maybe later, honey. I have to work on my physiotherapy exercises right now."

"Please, Daddy," she begged. "Just as far as Beaker Hill."

"Kristy, if I don't do my exercises, my leg will get stiff."

"Well, riding a horse is exercise, isn't it?"

Lester smiled. "How can I refuse with reasoning like that?"

With the aid of a stool, Lester was able to hoist himself behind Kristy. His injured leg was nearly pain-free, but its range of motion was limited. However, he felt good to be back in Whisper's saddle again.

The sun was rising, but it was still cold enough for the riders to see their breath in the air. Early morning dew covered the grassy green meadow, making the trek a little slippery, but the horse manoeuvred the terrain with agility.

As they neared Beaker Hill, the ground grew a little more precarious. The previous night's heavy rainfall had muddied the supporting rocks and gravel on the trail side of the hill. Lester knew it was too dangerous to go any farther, so he pulled on Whisper's reins to turn the horse around.

Suddenly, the earth gave way beneath them, sending the trio tumbling down the hillside. The sound of snapping

AT HEART

bones filled the air, immediately followed by the stallion's agonized whinny.

They landed in a gully partly filled with rainwater. Lester found himself pinned beneath Whisper's massive frame. Whisper lay on top of him in a crumpled heap, unable to move. Lester was completely immersed in water, and he pushed with all his strength to raise his head. His face broke the surface and he gulped in a large breath of air as he looked for his daughter.

"Kristy!" he yelled.

"I'm right here, Daddy," her voice called from the bank behind him.

"Are you okay, honey?"

"I think so. I just have a scratch on my knee."

"That's good, sweetie," he called. "I'm stuck under Whisper, and I need you to go and tell Mommy so she can get help."

"Are you and Whisper going to be okay, Daddy?" she cried.

"Yes, if you run home as fast as you can."

The muscles in Lester's neck were aching from the strain of keeping his head above water. He knew it would take Kristy at least half an hour to run home and that it would probably take another half hour for Penny to get a rescue team with a hoist. He would not be able to hold out that long; he felt exhausted already. He had to keep dropping his head into the water to rest his neck and then reemerge for air. His inspirations were weakening, and his whole body had gone numb from the icy water and lack of oxygen.

After many attempts to wriggle free, Lester gave up and tried to conserve his energy. Finally, after what seemed an eternity, he gave in to exhaustion and let his head sink beneath the water for the last time. He prayed to God that Kristy would remain home and not see his lifeless body pulled from the water. Once he had made peace with the fact that he was not going to make it, he awaited death in his shallow tomb.

Lester felt Whisper's snout nudge the side of his cheek, and he thought this was the horse's way of saying goodbye to him. Then he felt the horse burrow his own face into the water, placing his entire head beneath his rider's. This allowed Lester to break the surface again. He gasped air into his lungs.

He gulped as much air as he could, because he knew he would be dropped back into the water when Whisper came back up to breathe. He waited and waited, but the horse did not move. Lester rocked his head back and forth in an effort to rouse Whisper. Then he felt the horse's body shudder as it ran out of air, and Lester realized the sacrifice this great stallion had made for him. Tears streamed down his face, and the narrow gully echoed with the sound of his sobs.

* * *

AT HEART

A week later, the Barnett home was still a place of mourning as all members of the family grieved the loss of Whisper. However, one of the mares in the stable had given birth to a colt that morning. After a lot of coaxing, Lester was finally able to persuade Kristy to go and see the new pony. When she entered the stall and saw his dark coat and the little white crescent-shaped marking on his forehead, she smiled for the first time in a week.

"Why, he's just like Whisper!" she squealed in delight.

"I was hoping you'd see the resemblance, since this *is* Whisper's colt," Lester said with a grin. "Sam Davis told me about him, and I had him brought here. Would you like the task of naming him?"

"I sure would!"

"What would you like to call him?"

"Why, Whisper, of course," Kristy said.

Sunset Hill

LISA IVANY

IT WAS APRIL 2, 1945, in London, England, when Dr. Tom McBride washed up after ten straight hours of surgery. The dark circles etched under his blue eyes gave evidence to chronic lack of sleep. He removed his mask and cap, revealing a thick mass of black curls with flecks of grey, now plastered to his sweat-soaked head. Even in his present state, at the age of fifty-two, Tom still retained his boyish good looks. Most of the hospital's female personnel would have jumped at the chance to date the handsome and charming Dr. Tom McBride, but he seemed oblivious to their overtures.

The object of Tom's desire was Lynette Chafe, the young nurse from Petty Harbour, Newfoundland, who had joined their team two years ago. She had just graduated from nursing school and decided to use her newly acquired skills to help the Allies of

AT HEART

World War II. There was a shortage of nurses in Europe at the time and Lynette was one of many new recruits from Newfoundland who had enlisted to help the cause.

Her hair hung in long strawberry-blond waves around her oval face. Her sparkling emerald green eyes were what first captured Tom's attention. When she flashed her beautiful smile, she captured his heart.

She probably thinks of me as a father figure, he thought, noting their twenty-seven-year age difference. He would certainly never let her know his true feelings, or he would risk losing the close friendship they shared.

She was cleaning up in the sink next to him, and he thought it sad that she was spending her twenty-fifth birthday rinsing blood from her delicate hands instead of being home in Newfoundland, celebrating with her family and friends. He felt she should have stayed on the other side of the Atlantic Ocean and kept herself out of harm's way, but he knew her strong yearning to make a difference in people's lives where it was needed most. He shared the same desire and determination.

"What are your plans for your birthday?" he asked.

"I guess I'll just get cleaned up and go down to the cafeteria for dinner after my shift."

"Mind if I join you?"

She smiled. "I'd love it."

* * *

By the end of the workday, both doctor and nurse were ready to collapse. The cafeteria was packed with medical staff and ambulatory patients, and there were no spare tables available. Exhausted from being on their feet in the operating room all day, they both agreed they didn't have the energy or inclination to wait in line, choosing instead to go back to Tom's quarters so he could prepare a birthday dinner for her.

The crisp spring air energized the two, and by the time they reached Tom's flat, their fatigue had completely dissipated. Tom refused Lynette's help in the kitchen, insisting that it was her birthday and he wanted her to relax. She watched him prepare dinner and was pleasantly surprised to see how adept he was in the kitchen.

After a hearty dinner of shepherd's pie, Tom and Lynette unwound on the sofa and spoke of their respective homes. She described the fishing community of Petty Harbour, with its houses built on grassy hills overlooking the inlet. She came from a family of fishermen, her father and three brothers making their living on the water. It was hard work, but they never seemed to mind, and she and her mother would watch for their return each morning and breathe a sigh of relief when they motored back safely into the harbour.

Tom admitted to his own yearning for home back in Salthill, Ireland. He had inherited his family's 300-acre estate when he was in his early twenties and had made a prosperous business out of the riding stables and sheep farm. It was enough to support him through medical school, and he knew it was now being well looked after by his sister, Maureen.

"The pasture land is bright green and looks as thick and soft as a carpet," he said as he described his estate to Lynette. "My favourite spot is at the very back of the land, where I used to play with Maureen and my best friend, Paddy, when we were growing up. The edge of the cliff stretches to the sky, and when you look at it from a certain angle at sunset, it looks like two separate suns are setting, one on each side of the hill. Shades of pink, blue, and violet cover the sky. That's why we nicknamed it Sunset Hill."

"It must be beautiful," Lynette said.

"Yeah, it is. Best of all is that the land runs parallel to Galway Bay. There is nothing more breathtaking than watching the sun set over the water from that spot. Paddy even said that, when he dies, he wants to be buried there so he can enjoy eternity near the most beautiful sunsets in the world."

"Where's Paddy now?"

"I'm not sure. The last I heard, he was headed for the front lines. He's a major in the military and I can assure you, if his men are in the midst of battle, he's right up front with them, leading the charge. I pray for his safety every day."

"Sounds like you two are still close."

"He's the closest I've ever had to a brother. Even though he's a year younger than me, I've always looked up to him.

Paddy has this strength of character and serenity about him that keeps him calm in the most stressful of circumstances. Nobody ruffles his feathers, and he can find humour in almost any situation, which is why everyone adores him."

"I hope I get to meet him someday."

"When this war is over, you'll have to come to Ireland and do just that."

Tom's heart raced at the thought of having Lynette come home with him, even though his head was telling him to smarten up. This young girl would never fall for someone who was old enough to be her father. If only he could stop his torturous desire for this woman who had unwittingly laid claim to his heart.

The lateness of the hour, coupled with the long day in surgery, were taking their toll on Lynette. Her eyelids drooped and, after several attempts to stay alert, she finally succumbed to exhaustion and fell asleep on his sofa. Tom didn't have the heart to disturb her, but he wanted to make sure she was comfortable for the night. Sliding one hand behind her back and another beneath her knees, he carried her to his bedroom.

He gently tucked her between the sheets on his bed and pulled a blanket up to her chin. *I shouldn't have kept her up so late*, he thought, but he certainly didn't regret their evening together. As he left the room, he couldn't resist the temptation to turn for one more glance at her sleeping form. She looked so small and vulnerable in his bed, and he felt a strong urge to wrap himself protectively around her. *If only I were twenty-five years younger . . . or even twenty*, he thought despondently. Then everything would be different.

Tom spent the rest of the night tossing and turning on the sofa. When he closed his eyes, all he could visualize was Lynette's green eyes, her soft rosy lips . . . lips he wanted to claim with his own. Then a thought struck him. What if she had feelings for him as well? His thoughts drifted back to earlier in the evening, when they were sitting on the sofa and she was looking up into his eyes with complete interest and hanging onto his every word. She had shifted her weight, wedging her arm next to his, and she made no attempt to move it. Was it a deliberate manoeuvre?

By morning, Tom had made a decision to tell Lynette how he felt about her and let the chips fall where they may. Sure, she would probably reject him in a gracious manner, but if there was any chance at all that she could have feelings for him, he needed to find out.

"Tom, wake up!" Lynette called.

"What?" he asked sleepily, trying to open his heavy lids.

She shook him by the shoulder. "Wake up!"

"What's up?" he asked, now wide awake.

"The siren has been blaring for the last five minutes. We're needed at the hospital," she responded. "You must have been really tired to have slept through that."

They arrived at the hospital minutes later to await the incoming casualties. But instead of the usual large influx of wounded, the medics only carried in one stretcher. The stillness of the patient made Tom wonder if he was DOA.

"Where are the rest?" he asked.

"There are no others," one of the medics replied. "There were no survivors from the blitz this morning, except for this poor guy. He's more dead than alive, by the looks of him."

Tom and Lynette checked the soldier's vitals and found a very thready pulse at best. His face and hair were blackened with smoke and blood and the all too familiar stench of burnt flesh wafted from his body. The gauze dressing wrapped around his head was doing little to suppress the oozing of blood from his right temple. Lynette removed the dressing and cleaned the deep gash, and while she waited for Tom to suture the wound, she searched for the soldier's identification.

She found his dog tags and read, "His name is Major Patrick Brendan Doyle."

"Oh my God!" Tom exclaimed. He leaned down and studied the man's face. He said, "It's Paddy! I didn't recognize him under all this black soot."

"Is this the friend you told me about last night?" Lynette asked.

Visibly shaken, he could only manage to nod in response. A hard lump constricted his throat. Composing himself, he finished the physical examination of his best friend. Not only did Paddy have a severe concussion, but he had suffered extensive burns to his lower limbs, a fracture to his left ankle, and from the sounds Tom heard through the stethoscope, there was a possibility of a punctured lung. However, this would be easier to assess when, and if, the patient regained consciousness.

After his shift, Tom stayed by Paddy's bedside throughout the night, and by the time Lynette arrived for work the next morning, he had not slept a wink. Paddy had still not awakened. Lynette insisted that he leave to get some sleep, or he would be of little use to anyone. She promised to keep constant vigil over his dear friend in his absence and to notify him immediately if Paddy's condition deteriorated.

When Tom returned to the hospital, he was relieved to hear the sound of Paddy's laughter mingled with Lynette's as he neared his friend's cubicle. He whipped open the curtain that surrounded the bed.

"I'm glad to see you're not as dead as I thought," Tom said.

"I couldn't let you off that easy," Paddy countered. "You still owe me a steak dinner at McGuinney's Pub for the last time I slaughtered you at darts."

"Well, I guess the concussion didn't wipe out your memory," Tom laughed. "Now, on a more serious note, are you having much pain?"

"Not since I looked into the emerald eyes of this sweet angel and was reminded of the beautiful hills of Ireland."

Lynette laughed. "It's more likely due to the large dose of morphine I gave him."

Tom performed a thorough examination of Paddy and breathed a sigh of relief to find his lungs were clear. Several ribs were fractured, but they would mend with a little R and R, and Paddy's positive attitude would undoubtedly speed his recovery.

With a shortage of surgeons, Tom's time with his friend was quite limited, but Lynette's schedule permitted her more time to care for their favourite patient. Indeed, she and Paddy had become instant friends. Tom was happy to see two of the people he loved most in the world getting along so famously.

He was so wrapped up with work and spending his rare off-duty hours with Paddy that he decided to delay telling Lynette how he truly felt about her. There would be ample opportunity to tell her once Paddy had recuperated and was medically discharged.

By the last week of April, Paddy's diligence with his rehab program paid off, and he was able to walk without the aid of crutches. He still used a cane in his left hand for support, but most of the time he had his arm wrapped around Lynette's shoulder. It was quite obvious that he preferred her assistance to that of the cane. The burns on his legs would leave permanent scars, but the pain had lessened substantially and he never complained.

AT HEART

Since Paddy's recovery was going so well, he would soon be able to report for duty, albeit with a new company since he had lost all his men in the last battle. Although Tom dreaded the thought of his friend returning to fight, he was also anxious to have Lynette back to himself and finally reveal how he felt about her. He had been feeling a little left out lately. Although he would never begrudge his friend anything, a little prickle of jealousy was starting to raise its ugly head. He brushed the thought aside and knew that Lynette was just one of many people who easily made friends with Paddy.

"We have exciting news!" Paddy exclaimed, while holding Lynette's hand one morning.

"What news would that be?" Tom asked.

"We're engaged!"

"What? How did that happen?"

Lynette chimed in. "We've been spending a lot of time together and found that we have a lot in common. At some point we just fell in love."

"Well, congratulations," Tom uttered, trying to sound excited for the couple, though he felt as if a hot poker had just speared his midsection. "When's the big date?"

"We'll wait until the war is over and life returns to normal," Paddy replied. "I want to give her a big emerald ring to match her eyes, but for now she will have to settle for my lucky golden eagle pin." He transferred the object from his chest pocket to Lynette's uniform collar. Tom knew how much the pin meant to Paddy. His mother had given it to him as a good luck charm when he enlisted. His grandfather had worn the very same pin every day in the First World War, and he credited the talisman for his survival.

The call of duty for Paddy came shortly after his engagement. Tom had kept him secure in the hospital longer than was actually necessary, and the top brass were breathing down his neck. He could no longer justify his friend's hospital stay, and so released him to resume active duty, with the promise to keep an eye on his beautiful fiancée while he was away.

It broke Tom's heart to see Lynette's sorrowful eyes each day after Paddy's departure. He observed her tense expression whenever new casualties arrived. She would not relax until she had searched every face to ensure that Paddy was not among the wounded. The process was taking a heavy toll on her physically, as evidenced by her wan complexion and apparent weight loss. Emotionally, she was withdrawing from her friends and colleagues at the hospital. Tom would often find her sobbing and wrap his comforting arms about her shoulders.

He regretted not revealing his feelings to Lynette sooner. He feared the timing wasn't right and the age difference would be a problem, but she had fallen in love with an older man anyway, and now he had lost his chance. If only he had spoken up when he first realized the depth of his feelings; then, perhaps, the woman of his dreams would be his and she would not be worrying about her new fiancé. He would have fought relentlessly to win her heart if she had been engaged to anybody else in the world . . . but she was his best friend's girl, and he would never do anything to hurt either of them.

May 8, 1945 heralded victory in Europe when Germany surrendered unconditionally to the Allies. Bells rang out, and the streets of London were filled with people rejoicing and hugging one another. Inside the hospital, the mood was the highest it had ever been, as patients and staff cheered the end of the war. Even Lynette managed a beaming smile with this news.

On the afternoon of May 12, the majority of the wounded soldiers had been dispatched home and Tom and Lynette enjoyed a rare quiet break together in the empty staff lounge.

"I wonder why it's taking Paddy so long to return," she sighed.

"Don't worry. He'll be back for you as soon as he's able," Tom reassured her. "He has to make arrangements for his men to go home first."

Lynette, satisfied with his explanation, visibly relaxed into her seat.

"Dr. McBride!" an orderly called from the doorway. "You and Nurse Chafe are needed in emergency."

When Tom and Lynette arrived at the ER, they could feel the change in the ward's atmosphere even before they saw the downcast faces of the staff. Over the previous four days, everyone had been in high spirits, celebrating the end of the war. However, that feeling was now overshadowed by a dark cloud. The nursing staff looked away, not able to make eye contact with either of them, but Dr. Grant, the other ER physician on duty, met them with a sympathetic look and pointed to the end of the ward.

Reluctantly, Tom led Lynette to the curtained-off stretcher indicated by his colleague. They arrived just in time to see a sheet being pulled over the lifeless eyes of Paddy Doyle. Tom was able to catch Lynette before she hit the floor in a dead faint.

Tom managed to keep busy for the next few days, between consoling Lynette and making arrangements for Paddy's service, to be held back home in Ireland. He tried not to deal with his own grief. He had to stay strong for Lynette's sake; she was not handling the situation well at all and blamed herself, saying she had the golden eagle pin which would have kept Paddy safe. Tom tried to comfort her and said that, with or without the pin, Paddy would still not have survived the shrapnel wound that killed him.

AT HEART

The service was held five days later at Sunset Hill. The large gathering of mourners sent Paddy off with military honours for his bravery in the war and sang his favourite songs of Ireland. Tom stood with one hand in a salute as tears filled his eyes. His other arm pulled Lynette close and she hugged him tightly, letting her own tears flow down her ashen face.

With the end of war, Tom and Lynette terminated their positions in England and stayed on at the McBride Estate in Ireland. Tom eventually returned to his medical practice in one of Galway's private clinics, but Lynette had no wish to resume her nursing career. She didn't have the heart for it anymore, as she could not erase all the pain and suffering she had seen on the soldiers' faces in her two years of service in London. Though she felt guilty for not moving back to her home in Petty Harbour with her family, she knew she would not be able to tolerate the pity she would see in everyone's eyes. She needed some time on her own.

The most haunting of all was the image of Paddy's face, covered with blood, a gaping wound where his forehead had once been, above his cold and lifeless eyes.

Maureen was a lifeline for Lynette. She involved her in the riding business to create a diversion from her mourning. It was easy to see the family resemblance between Maureen and Tom. She was ten years younger than her brother, but had the same tall, lean build, thick curly dark hair, and kind, grey-blue eyes.

Maureen adored her brother and was happy to have him back home, safe from the horrors of war, but she noticed a change in him. Oftentimes she would see him gaze off into space, not speaking or moving for long periods of time. She knew something was troubling him.

"A penny for your thoughts, big brother," Maureen said to Tom in the den early one morning.

"I don't think my thoughts are worth a penny these days."

"I wouldn't say that if they're about Lynette," she persisted.

"What do you mean?"

"You're in love with her, aren't you?"

"Is it that obvious?" he asked.

"It is to me, but I know you better than just about anyone. I know you're hurting from the loss of Paddy, like the rest of us. But your grief runs deeper. Have you ever told her how you feel?"

"It was never the right time. And then she met Paddy."

"Why don't you tell her now?"

"She's grieving for the man she was about the marry. It's definitely not the right time now."

"I wouldn't be so sure," she remarked over her shoulder as she left to go to the stables.

AT HEART

Tom wondered if Lynette had said something to make Maureen believe there was a chance for them. The two women had become very close, and Lynette seemed to be opening up to his sister. However, it would be crude to approach a woman in mourning. It was not the right time, regardless of how much he loved her. He was a gentleman, after all. Tom was satisfied to have her living under the same roof and to take their daily strolls which always landed them at Sunset Hill.

One evening in July, Tom and Lynette sat on a grassy knoll overlooking Galway Bay and watched the pink sky give way to night. They were sitting on a blanket, and the wind blowing over the water had a bit of a nip to it, so Tom wrapped his jacket around her shoulders. The tender gesture was not lost on Lynette, and she leaned forward, gently brushing his lips with her own. Startled, he drew back. He thought she had meant it only as a symbol of friendship. However, he was astonished when she locked him with a sensuous stare and slid her hand behind his neck. He was spellbound by her eyes, and a force he could no longer resist pushed his mouth to her honeyed lips for a lingering kiss. Under a canopy of millions of twinkling stars, two yearning bodies reached for each other in shared pain, loneliness, and desire.

* * *

For the next two weeks, they spent every waking hour together. Tom's heart soared as he finally revealed his true feelings to Lynette, and even though he knew she still loved Paddy, he felt, in time, she would possibly fall in love with him.

By mid-August, Tom gained his courage and asked, "Lynette, would you ever consider becoming my wife? I know you still love Paddy, and I don't expect to replace him in your heart, but I'd settle for second place. You don't have to answer me now, but just think about it, okay?"

"Let's get married right away," she said.

"Are you serious?"

"Yes, I've never been more serious. Let's have the service on Sunset Hill."

Within a week, Lynette Chafe became Mrs. Tom McBride. It was a small ceremony, with Maureen as Lynette's matron of honour, and Maureen's husband, Rory, as Tom's best man. Standing at his favourite spot, overlooking beautiful Galway Bay, Tom felt sad not having Paddy by his side on his wedding day. However, the pain eased a little more each time he looked into the lovely face of his new bride.

The next morning, the mood in the house was jovial. Lynette's eyes were still sad, but there was a noticeable degree of improvement. A letter from her mother arrived later that day.

As she read the letter, Lynette began to cry. Between sobs, she explained to Tom and Maureen that her father and all three of her brothers had been killed in the war. Their bodies had only recently been found, when an abandoned prison camp had been discovered in Germany. There were no survivors.

"Tom, I must go home to Petty Harbour. I'm the only one my mother has left. She must be devastated back there alone," she cried.

"Of course, you must go," he replied.

"I'll make the arrangements to get you on a flight right away," Maureen offered.

"Make that two plane tickets, Maureen," Tom added. "I'm going with her."

"What about your practice?" Lynette asked.

"You're more important right now."

They flew into Torbay Airport two days later and hired a taxi to take them to Petty Harbour. It was nearly midnight when they arrived at the Chafe home, and Lynette was embraced tightly in her mother's welcoming arms. Stella Chafe had the same green eyes as her daughter, but that's where the resemblance ended. She was a short, plump woman with an oval face, and her snow-white hair was secured tightly in a bun.

The aftermath of the war's pain and suffering on the survivors was never more evident to Tom as it was at that moment. Tears welled in his own eyes as he watched the two women clinging to each other. The souls of the valiant soldiers who lost their lives during the war were now at peace, but as Tom watched his wife and her mother, he wondered if there were any real victors of the war.

The women pulled apart, and Lynette introduced her mother to her new husband. Although Stella was shocked that her daughter had married, she quickly embraced her new son-in-law and welcomed him to the family. She put the kettle on the stove and set the table with a variety of breads, biscuits, and cheese, showing Tom some of that famous Newfoundland hospitality.

The following day, Lynette gave Tom a walking tour of Petty Harbour. Strolling along the rocky shoreline hand in hand with his young bride, Tom was repeatedly welcomed by locals who came out of their homes to greet him. Everyone wanted the handsome Irish doctor to come in for a cup of tea, which he promised them all he would do soon. By evening, he felt a sense of belonging to Newfoundland, as though he were back home in Ireland.

From the front veranda of Stella's bungalow, nestled into the hillside next to the harbour, Tom and Lynette watched the sun set over the horizon. It filled him with a sense of peace and contentment, as though it were sinking into Galway Bay from Sunset Hill. He decided then that he would stay in Newfoundland.

During the postwar era, the economy was at an all-time low, and although Tom had a considerable income from his estate in Salthill, he did not draw upon it to establish his medical clinic in Petty Harbour. He thought it would be in poor taste to reveal his wealth when the area residents had so little. He preferred to treat his patients in the back room of the two-storey home he had just purchased, situated on the water's edge. Rarely was there money to pay for his services, but the patients kept his pantry stocked with eggs, fish, wild game, and an endless supply of baked goods.

The McBrides appeared to be the sweetest of couples in the community. He loved his wife more with each passing year, although the happy girl he had met in England never resurfaced. She constantly reassured him of her love and was quite a passionate lover, but he knew her heart belonged to Paddy and probably always would.

Their only child, Brigid, was growing up fast, and Tom wondered if Lynette would have been happier with more children. After some complications during her delivery, Lynette had to undergo an emergency hysterectomy. Tom reassured his wife that he was quite happy to have one child, but he would often see a look of despair in her eyes when she didn't know he was watching her. Those episodes were usually short-lived, as their beautiful green-eyed daughter, a small replica of herself, would find some mischief to get into that needed her mother's attention.

Years later, when Brigid turned seventeen and received her acceptance for nursing school, her mother was somewhat anxious. The images of the maimed and dying soldiers still haunted her at times and, of course, her final view of Paddy's lifeless face would be forever etched in her mind. However, she placed things in perspective and reminded herself that they were no longer at war. Certainly, there would be times during Brigid's career when she would be exposed to seriously injured patients, and even death, but Lynette admired her daughter's strong will and knew she could handle anything she put her mind to.

"Mom, I was trying on your old nursing uniform and I found this pin on one of the collars," Brigid said as she passed the outfit to her mother.

"The golden eagle pin," she whispered. "I had forgotten about it."

"Is it special?"

She smiled. "It was a long time ago. I'd like to keep it."

She extracted the pin that at one time had served as a substitute for an engagement ring and thought back to the good times she and Tom had shared with Paddy in London. The mood in the wartime hospital seemed brighter when the threesome were together, and it had never been the same after Paddy died.

Little by little, Brigid had been packing the items she would need to stay in residence at the nursing school over the summer. Her parents would travel with her to see her settled in, and then return to Newfoundland without her. They had plane tickets to Halifax, dated August 28, 1962, but they would never be used, due to Lynette's sudden illness.

AT HEART

It had started as a tiny lump in her left breast which she had ignored for months until it had increased to the size of a marble, and she finally sought medical attention. After a biopsy, she was found to have malignant cancer. When it was decided she would have a mastectomy, it was too late. The cancer had spread to her lymph nodes and could not be successfully treated.

The outcome was inevitable, so Lynette declined any measures that would prolong her life and make her sicker in the process. She preferred to die with as much dignity as she could, and lessen the time her husband and daughter would have to watch her suffer. When the pain became unbearable, she was admitted to hospital and agreed to the administration of morphine, knowing she was in the final stage of her illness.

When they were alone in Lynette's small hospital room, she turned to her husband. "Tom, there is something I want you to do for me," she murmured haltingly in her weakened state.

"What's that, my love?"

"Make sure Brigid goes to nursing school."

"I will, and you'll be home soon to make sure she does," he said, with tears in his eyes.

With tremendous strain, she whispered, "Honey, you don't have to pretend with me. I know I'm going to die." Catching her breath, she continued, "I've made peace with that, but you have to accept it, too."

The energy required to talk had drained Lynette, and her

head rolled to one side as she slipped into an exhausted sleep. Tom stared down at her pasty complexion and wasted form, remembering the bright and vibrant woman she had been just a short time ago. While she lay sleeping, his resolve finally let go and the tears he had been holding back poured down his face.

Lynette's fingers twitched slightly, and he looked into her eyes. Once they had been a sparkling shade of emerald green, but now they seemed faded and cold. Her lips pursed to speak, but no sound was uttered. She tried again, and Tom put his ear to her lips.

"Sunset Hill," was all she managed before falling into a sleep from which she would never awaken. Tom gave her mouth one final kiss and drew her lifeless body up into his arms. He rocked her back and forth in his arms, letting the tears flow for the woman he had loved for so many years and who, in death, still loved another man.

On the day Lynette was laid to rest, dark clouds gathered overhead and a cold mist from Galway Bay sprayed the mourners at Sunset Hill. Tom's baritone voice sang,

> "If you ever go across the seas to Ireland,
> Then maybe at the closing of your day,
> You will sit and watch the moon rise over Claddagh,
> And watch the sun go down on Galway Bay."

AT HEART

He sang the remaining verses haltingly as tears fell from his eyes. He and Brigid joined hands in a silent prayer of farewell. They mourned the loss of a wife and mother whom they cherished and would never see again this side of Heaven.

Brigid clasped the golden eagle pin in her hand and asked, "Dad, why did you decide to bury mom at the same place as Paddy? She was *your* wife, after all."

She was never mine, Tom thought. *Oh, she may have honoured me by taking my name, but Paddy captured her heart a long time ago and never let it go.*

He replied, "This was your mother's favourite place on earth because we were married here. One day I'll be buried here as well."

Brigid nestled into his arms, satisfied with his response. They held each other in shared sorrow and love on that grey windy day at Sunset Hill.

One year later, Tom left his home in Petty Harbour and returned to visit his Irish estate. This would surely be his last time crossing the Atlantic, due to a heart condition. There had been a dramatic decline in the good doctor's health since the passing of his precious Lynette, as though he were slowly dying of a broken heart. He felt cheated, not only because she had died, but because with her last breath she had proven her love for another man. *Why else would she want to be laid next to Paddy?* he silently asked. After all their years of marriage, he had hoped he would be the one she truly loved.

He was so engrossed in his thoughts as he looked over Galway Bay that he didn't notice his sister's presence until she looped her arm through his.

"You still miss her, don't you?"

"With every beat of my heart," he murmured.

"She was a very special lady and she really loved you," Maureen said. "I told her a long time ago that you, like Paddy, wished to be buried at Sunset Hill when your time on earth came to a close. She immediately told me she shared the same desire because she wanted her spirit to remain here with yours for eternity."

"I never knew," he moaned.

Tom felt a cold breeze from the spot Maureen had vacated. She had sensed his need for solitude as he gazed through misted eyes to the water below. Then the realization hit him . . . Lynette's spirit lingered here on the coast of Galway Bay, waiting for *him* to join her for eternity. She was not here to be reunited with Paddy, after all.

For all their years together, he felt he had been competing with the ghost of his dead friend, but now he discovered that what he was actually fighting was his own insecurity. He had never truly believed his wife whenever she told him she loved him, thinking she was just saying it because she thought he needed to hear it. He thought she had just settled for him as the consolation prize because she couldn't have the man she really wanted.

In a matter of moments his emotions went from confusion to grief to anger. He didn't know if he was angrier at Lynette for not having made him realize her true feelings years ago or at himself for being a blind fool. A melancholy settled over him for the life he knew he had wasted on self-doubt, when he could have been truly happy. Now it was too late. He knelt by her grave and mumbled, "Why didn't I see how much you loved me?"

He closed his eyes and visualized the girl with the beautiful emerald eyes who still held his heart. At that moment, a whisper of warm air brushed the side of his face, as though he had been kissed by a ghost. Tom felt a searing pain that ripped through his chest and brought him to his knees. He knew the beating of his heart was coming to an inescapable halt as he lay immobile on top of Lynette's grave, but he was not afraid: he was about to spend eternity with the woman he loved and who truly loved him.

Danny Wonder

ROBERT HUNT

Memories crowd Jeff Duggan's mind as he looks out through his windshield at the hard rain. A small rumble echoes from the distant sky as grey-white clouds move together to blot out the once blue sky. The wind has just started to change direction, moving toward the east, as the remaining days of spring fade into oblivion.

Cool weather coming, Jeff thinks as he bundles himself in his coat against the weather. He turns the car heater up another notch, then nestles deep into his seat, drifting back to another time.

He stirs and looks to his right, sifts through the softball photographs on the seat beside him. He does that sometimes; he would just get in his car, take a coffee and his photographs with him, and drive to the ballpark. His favourite

AT HEART

parking spot is behind the rusted metal fence, and there he would stare at the baseball diamond he once coached on.

Jeff looks at the ballfield and smiles at what he had accomplished. Through the misty haze on the open field he can see the shadows of the many kids he had coached over the years, those whom have grown into adulthood. He sees Billy Townsend making that big catch and tagging out an opposing player at second; he can see tall, slim Bert "Bunky" Long track down a fly ball that seems destined for the right-field fence, but is caught moments before it can drop out of sight. He witnesses another great performance by his sure-handed catcher, Bobby Reid, as he spreads his arms to catch a ball that would have been missed by any other catcher in the league. Jeff also sees his assistant coach and best friend, Mike Strong, who has since passed away, teaching the kids softball techniques with a big heart and unbridled enthusiasm. A heartache of memories flood back to him as he sits in his car with only the rain for company.

The sound of excited youngsters still rings in his ears. Young boys are running the bases, catching fly balls, throwing the softball to one another. His teammates are telling jokes, the crowd is settling into their seats. The smell of the park, the hot dogs, popcorn, all these things invade his senses.

And the crowd! He can still hear the crowd, the laughter, the cheers with every pitch, the boos when the opposing players got a hit, and the extended cheers when they struck out.

Jeff singles out one photograph, one in which he is being embraced by a team of young boys who had just won their first league championship. This photo holds first place in his heart. It shows one boy in particular rushing to greet him with his hand extended in a handshake and a face blossomed with the smile that once lit up this ballfield.

Though retired now and no longer coaching, Jeff Duggan's mind races back in time, twelve years before, to the league championship, when a young, one-armed boy taught him all the lessons in life he needed to know. A young man who surprised him with his attitude toward life, and what he wanted and needed to be whole again—just to play ball. This young boy touched him like no other ball player has ever done.

It is June 24, 1992, in Fortune, Newfoundland. Jeff Duggan is fifty-five years old, a coach who has dedicated his life to teaching young ball players the fundamentals of the game. Softball is just a game, he preached, in which the main objective is to have fun, and the kids on Jeff's team are young men dedicated to sportsmanship who know the meaning of teamwork and how to work as individuals toward a greater goal. He wants these kids to learn that cooperating with others extends itself into how you conduct yourself in life.

With this team approach in mind, he looks in the dugout

and sees young Danny LeGrow. The boy is sitting at the end of the bench, his eyes on the kids playing ball out on the field. Danny doesn't say much, but his eyes follow every movement of the game. He has a drive that few kids his age possess. The intensity in his eyes is what all coaches, including Jeff, wish they could bottle.

It doesn't seem to bother Danny that he was born with a disability. It's all he knows. What bothers him is that he cannot play the game he loves so much. The boy had been born with only one arm.

Jeff has just started coaching the Fortune Bay Monarchs in their first year, and he doesn't know Danny very well. The boy is something of a clubhouse fixture; the last coach had allowed him to sit and watch the game as long as he wanted. Danny watches because he wants to be close to the game. It can't be easy for a fifteen-year-old boy. It must be like owning a bike that has no wheels. But he enjoys watching and seems to play every game in his mind. He analyzes aspects of the game that other players pay no attention to, like what opposing players do, how they pitch, hit, and run. He sees their weaknesses and their strengths. The boy takes it all in, but nobody ever asks his opinion. He just sits there and watches.

But soon, a twist of fate and Jeff's assistant coach, Mike, will change all that. Jeff will soon find out that there is more to Danny LeGrow than just a kid with one arm who sits on the end of the bench and takes notes.

They are five games into the season, with two wins and three losses, and today they are down 4-2. As Jeff looks down the row of players in the dugout, Danny catches his attention. The boy is busy writing down every pitch and swing by the opposing team. Jeff watches as Danny turns to say something to his mom, Crystal. She smiles that patient mom smile and nods back at him. The Monarchs struggle through the game, but despite their best efforts, they lose 5-2. As the players are packing up their equipment, Jeff walks to the end of the bench, where Danny sits with his mother.

"Hi, Mrs. Legrow," he says. "It seems Danny has a great love for the game."

Crystal LeGrow smiles. She says softly, "He's always been like that, Mr. Duggan. From age five, Danny has had a passion for this game. He loves it so much, I wish to God that he could be like the other kids and just once have his chance to play."

Jeff looks from mother to son, and all he can think to say is, "So do I, Mrs. LeGrow, so do I."

Their conversation, though short, sticks with Jeff. He begins to think of ways he can include Danny in the game. For thirty years he has coached softball, and he is determined to come up with a way for Danny to realize his own dreams, as so many kids before him have under Jeff's tutelage. He decides to talk it over with Mike.

The next day, they ask Mrs. LeGrow for permission to see if they could get Danny to try his skills at swinging the bat and making contact with the ball. She says, "Ask Danny." When Mike approaches the boy with the idea, Danny jumps at the chance.

For several days, Mike and Jeff teach Danny how to swing. But, toward week's end, Danny finally says, "Thanks for trying, coaches, but as you can see I'm just not meant to play ball. Sorry if I let you guys down."

Mike looks at Jeff in shock. Here is this fifteen-year-old kid apologizing for not being able to swing a bat properly. Jeff is equally surprised.

Jeff smiles and says, "Danny, you have not let anyone down here. I promise you, Mr. Strong and I will find a way for you to play softball. Maybe coaching. How does that sound to you?"

Danny smiles that smile of his, nods, and heads home.

The next day, Jeff answers the phone at work. On the other end is an exuberant Mike who is talking so fast that Jeff has a hard time keeping up. Mike is laughing, trying to get what he has to say out in one mouthful.

"Jeff, you won't believe this. It's fantastic!"

"Mike, slow down. What are you trying to say?"

"My friend, meet me at the ball field and you will see something truly amazing. Hurry!"

Jeff, caught up in his friend's excitement, drives the three miles to the field in about five minutes. When he turns the corner, he sees that Mike was right. Here is Danny on the ball field, pitching the ball to Mike. Jeff stops and stands by his car, silently watching the boy's delivery. And it is beautiful! Straight down the middle! Danny's arm is like a machine. His velocity is outstanding. Here is a kid with one arm, throwing the ball to Mike at a good sixty to seventy miles per hour, and throwing ninety per cent of them for strikes! Jeff is overcome with joy. Mike has found what Danny is really good at—pitching!

Mike comes over to the fence and says with a bright smile, "Well, coach, what do you think? Can Danny try out for the team?"

Jeff laughs. "I think, my friend, that you are a genius. How did you find out he could pitch?"

"Actually, it was by luck. I was trying to get him to swing at a ball, and it skipped about twenty feet behind him. On instinct, I asked him to throw it back to me. He threw it back all right, at about fifty miles an hour! He's been sending fireballs at me for half an hour now."

Danny stares at the two men. With a shy smile he asks if he can try out for the team. Jeff nods and says that, if it's okay with Danny's mother, it's okay with them.

In the following days, Jeff and Mike discover that Danny has a remarkable memory for details about hitters. He knows how each one hits, swings, and what pitches they are good and bad at hitting.

They train Danny for weeks to pitch for the team when

he is needed, waiting for the right time to put him in the game. Finally, on a late Saturday evening in July, young Danny LeGrow gets the chance he has been waiting for all his life. This day will live on in Jeff's memory for a long time. The Monarchs are playing the Grand Bank Lions. They are leading 3-2, in the top of the fifth, when their starting pitcher, Luke Short, begins to tire. The Lions have runners on first and second, and no outs. Jeff calls a time out, walks to the end of the dugout, and stands in front of Danny. The boy's head is bowed and he doesn't look up as Jeff speaks.

"Well, Danny, what do you think? Now is your chance. Are you ready to pitch?"

Danny looks up at Jeff and, without saying a word, picks up his glove. He walks toward the mound. He draws another startled exchange between Jeff and Mike when he walks to the umpire and confers with him briefly. The umpire nods, then Danny walks around to each of his teammates' positions, and shakes their hands. He then looks skyward and says in a low voice, "This game is for you, Dad."

The crowd is silent as Danny walks back to the mound, composes himself, and waits for the catcher to give him his signs. Danny stares at him a moment, then delivers the first pitch. A strike! The crowd erupts. Jeff looks at the radar gun: 68 mph. Three minutes later, Danny has struck out the batter. He has amazed everyone with how he judged the batter and picked hm apart with his curve ball, his slider, and his blinding fast ball. His windup is poetry in motion, and his concentration is outstanding. With each pitch, the crowd cheers, "Danny Wonder, Danny Wonder! Go, Danny Wonder!" Fifth inning, three batters up, two strike-outs and a pop-up, inning six, two strike-outs and a ground out. At the top of the seventh, the Monarchs score another run and Danny walks to the mound for his last three outs. Before he throws, he looks at his mom, smiles at her, and again looks up in the sky. He turns his head toward Jeff Duggan and mouths the words *thank you*. Jeff looks at Mike, and though he will never admit it, tears stand in his assistant's eyes. *This is what I got into coaching for in the first place*, Jeff thinks. *This is what it's all about. To train kids into becoming men!*

Danny forces the first batter to ground out to second, strikes out the second batter, and gets a 2-2 pitch count on the third batter, Tommy Walsh. He calls for a time out, which is granted by the umpire. He walks over to Jeff and Mike in the dugout, and Jeff says, "Danny, how are you? Is your arm holding out okay?"

Danny smiles and says, "Today you gave me a chance to do something I never thought I could do. I will always be grateful to you both. I just wanted you guys to know that I will strike him out when I go back. He will chase the inside curve I have ready for him. Tommy always was a big sucker for that inside pitch. But before I strike him out, I want you to know that this pitch is for you."

Without another word, he turns around and returns to

AT HEART

the mound. He stares the batter down for a moment, takes the catcher's sign, and delivers an astounding 76 mph inside curve that takes Tommy unawares. The crowd goes wild, and Danny's teammates swarm to the mound and lift him up on their shoulders. Jeff hugs Mike tightly and they are both howling, laughing, and shouting in amazement and disbelief. Mrs. LeGrow races to the dugout and hugs the two men, and this moment will be etched in Jeff Duggan's mind twelve years from now, when he sits in his idling car in the pouring rain, reminiscing over his baseball cards and glory days gone by.

We won the game, Jeff thinks as he looks out over the rain-soaked ball field, *but even if we hadn't, it would still have been the best day of my coaching career as I looked at that kid's face, and I knew that would be a day I would never forget. That day, a young boy showed us all what the word dedication meant.*

Twelve years ago, on a late Saturday evening in July, Coach Duggan learned from a young boy what it takes to be a man.

Standoff at Widow's Peak

LISA IVANY

Red-tinged water flowed down the sink's drain as Monty Whalen scrubbed his trembling hands. His mother's dried blood was no longer evident, and his own skin was red and swollen as he moved the scrubbing brush harshly across his fingers and palms. Deeper and deeper he pressed the bristles, as though this action could erase the images of his recently slain mother.

"Come on!" Craig Dolan called from the hallway. "You've got to get out of here before they start looking for you."

Monty quickly dried his hands and grabbed the knapsack Craig had supplied with provisions for his late-night escape. Craig was the only person in the world Monty could trust now.

AT HEART

If only I had stayed at work, he thought. *This could have all been avoided*. He could see the headlines in tomorrow's paper already: "Troubled Teen Slays Mother and Escapes Justice."

"The map to Widow's Peak is in the small outside pocket of your pack," Craig said. "There's enough food in the main compartment to hold you over until I get there."

"Thanks for everything."

"No thanks necessary. I know you'd do it for me. Now one last thing . . . don't forget to ditch the car at the old abandoned tar pit."

"Are you sure no one will see it there?" Monty asked.

"Yes, I'm sure," Craig said. "Drive it deep into the woods behind the site and no one will find it." The two young men embraced before Monty crept through the side door and was swallowed up by the chilly night air.

Melanie Leyte studied the map on her desk, marking off the trail she would be hiking later in the day. Her job as a conservation officer in the Stephenville depot required her to work outside on the mountain ranges. She enjoyed her stints in the forest, but it was early May and she knew the trail was still carpeted with snow in many areas, making the terrain treacherous.

Ordinarily, her co-worker and fiancé, Drew Kelly, would be making the hike up to the wilderness station at Widow's Peak with her, but he had been called away to investigate an area of suspected moose poaching near Englee. The Department in Port Saunders had sent a fax, informing Melanie that their new recruit, Craig Dolan, would be reporting for duty on Monday morning, but she couldn't wait four days to go to Widow's Peak. Due to recent wind conditions and a shortage of staff, no one was able to make the trip to the station to replenish supplies. She felt she had no choice but to make the trip herself.

She donned her hiking boots, brown fleece-lined Forestry jacket, and gloves. The sun's warm rays shone through the window of her corner office, but she knew how cold it could get up in the mountains, especially at nightfall. Since it would take half a day to reach her destination, she knew she would have to stay until the next morning.

Melanie grabbed her matching brown wool cap and jammed it down over her flaxen waves. Stray wisps of hair peeked beneath her cap, ending just above big aquamarine eyes. She was quite an attractive girl, with a short perky nose and pink cheeks that always looked as though they had been kissed by the wind. Her youthful features continued to conceal her age of thirty-four years quite well.

The halfway point of the ten-mile trek was marked by a wooden shelter with a picnic table in its centre, surrounded by a thick wall of black spruce. It had been constructed by previous conservation officers as a place to rest and have a bite to eat for their regularly scheduled trips to Widow's Peak. This is where Melanie headed to have lunch.

AT HEART

She gave a little start when she saw movement inside the structure. She had not expected company.

A young man with curly, shoulder-length blond hair and soft blue eyes stared at her timidly. He looked as though he were more startled than Melanie, and his stance revealed his propensity for flight.

After the initial shock, Melanie noticed his Forestry uniform and quickly calmed down. Above his left chest pocket, in golden thread on his identification badge was stitched "C. Dolan."

"So, you're Craig Dolan, the new guy," she stated.

"Yes," he stammered.

"We weren't expecting you until Monday."

"I was able to get away earlier than expected, so I thought I'd check out the area."

"I'm heading to Widow's Peak as soon as I finish lunch," she said. "It's about five miles from here. You're welcome to join me if you like."

"Sounds great," said Craig.

The narrow path up the steep incline forced them to walk single file. Melanie led the way with her back to Craig, so she didn't notice the way his eyes constantly scanned the walkway and forest. She spent the next thirty minutes chatting amicably to her new co-worker, asking questions to make conversation and trying to find out a bit about him. His answers seemed evasive and as though they were being painstakingly extracted from him. She assumed he was a quiet sort and not much of a talker, but she had no problem keeping the conversation going herself. Once they reached the station and had a chance to unwind, he would probably be more at ease to talk. Melanie had a genuine interest in people, plants, animals, and indeed life itself, which her two brothers often teased her about. They said she could talk to a tree stump and discover all the secrets of the forest.

The higher they climbed, the quieter Melanie became, needing to conserve her energy to propel herself up the path. The mounds of snow grew thicker and more frequent as they passed through densely shaded areas of the trail that had not yet been thinned for the season. Finally, they topped the final ridge and saw a small wooden hut.

Melanie smiled. "Welcome to Widow's Peak."

"Why is it called Widow's Peak?" Craig asked.

"Come and I'll show you."

They walked into the station and Melanie went to the large window at the back that overlooked a huge valley. A rounded area of rocky terrain stretched about fifty feet from the building and then abruptly ended.

When Craig reached Melanie's side, she said, "See how the ground just drops straight down for hundreds of feet?"

"Yeah."

"Many hunters have fallen to their deaths from that ledge because they came upon it before they saw it, especially in foggy weather. In deference to the women who have lost their husbands at this place, it has been named Widow's Peak."

AT HEART

"That's sad," Craig murmured.

"Yes it is. The station was purposely erected on this spot with solar panels to reveal the edge of the cliff. There hasn't been a single death since this place was built two years ago. It's mostly used now as a safe haven for misguided hikers or hunters. We keep it supplied with firewood and food to help them out until they get redirected or rescued."

While Melanie stocked the shelves with provisions, Craig went outside to the large bin to gather wood. He cautiously surveyed his surroundings, staring intently into the darkest hollows of trees as though waiting for someone or something to spring from their depths. Satisfied there was no imminent danger, he quickly piled his arms with birch junks and returned to the shelter. Upon opening the door, he heard a news bulletin on the kitchen radio.

"Warning to all citizens. Please be on the lookout for Monty Whalen, who is wanted by the RCMP in connection with the death of his foster mother, Jessie Ellsworth. He was last seen heading east from Stephenville on the Trans-Canada Highway. Mr. Whalen is nineteen years of age, 5'10", 165 pounds, with blond curly hair, blue eyes, and a tattoo of a cross behind his left ear. He is considered armed and dangerous."

Craig darted across the room to the kitchen counter and flicked off the radio's switch just as the announcer said, "When last seen, Mr. Whalen was wearing . . ."

Melanie spun around with a questioning look in her eyes.

"Sorry," Craig apologized. "But I find the news so depressing, don't you?"

"It can be, but it's nice to stay informed," she countered. "For instance, we should keep a lookout for that guy they just mentioned on the radio. I wouldn't want to meet up with him."

"That's typical," he snarled. "You've decided the guy is guilty before even hearing his side of the story."

"Well, I imagine if the police are looking for him, they must have a pretty good reason, and they *did* say he was armed and dangerous."

"Don't believe everything you hear from the media or the police," he argued.

"They have a responsibility to tell the truth," Melanie persisted. "Besides, the fact that he's on the run makes him look guilty, don't you think?"

"I'm sure he has his reasons. Let's just forget about it."

Melanie prepared dinner and Craig lit the kindling in the fireplace. The station quickly filled with the sound of crackling wood, and the cold was soon replaced by a cozy warmth from the fire.

Although not a man of many words, Craig proved to be an enthusiastic cribbage player. He visibly relaxed after consuming a couple of glasses of brandy that evening, and Melanie watched this transformation, noticing the occasional smile which lit up his face and put a sparkle in his otherwise sombre eyes. She had been trying unsuccessfully all day to break through his stern facade and was delighted to see a charming young man emerging.

They both retired early as the effects of the long hike and the alcohol took their toll; Melanie to the lone bedroom and Craig to the davenport in the main room. It wasn't long before Melanie fell into an exhausted sleep. She was awakened by the sound of ringing, and as she reluctantly pulled herself from a pleasant dream, she realized it was the radio phone next to her bed.

"Hello," she mumbled sleepily.

"Hi, honey." Drew's voice spoke at the other end. "Did I wake you?"

"Yes, but that's okay. It's nice to hear your voice."

"I'm still in Englee, but I'll be home tomorrow night. I just wanted to check on you because of the news broadcast about Monty Whalen. Did you hear about it?"

"Yeah, he's the suspect the police are looking for."

"I'm glad you didn't go to Widow's Peak with that guy out there somewhere."

"Actually, I *am* at Widow's Peak," Melanie responded, "but I'm not alone."

"Who went with you?"

"The new guy, Craig Dolan."

"That's impossible, Melanie."

"What do you mean?"

"Craig Dolan has to write his final exam in Stephenville tomorrow before he is qualified to start working over here next week."

"But . . . he's here."

"What does he look like?"

"He has blue eyes and curly blond hair. He looks exactly like that actor, Christopher Atkins."

"Melanie, I've met Craig Dolan, and he has straight, coal-black hair. The person you just described is definitely not him."

"So, if that's not Craig Dolan sleeping out on the sofa, who is it? Oh my God!"

"Let's not jump to conclusions just yet, honey. However, I do want you to lock the bedroom door and stay there until I can get help to you. Whatever you do, don't reveal that you suspect anything."

"Okay, Drew. Just hurry," Melanie whispered anxiously.

When she terminated the call, she tiptoed to the bedroom door and pressed her ear against it in an effort to hear if Craig (or Monty, or whoever he was) had been listening outside. She couldn't hear any movement, but she was sure she heard low snoring. At least, she thought, she was not in immediate danger.

She thought back to the news bulletin on the radio and how they had described Monty Whalen with curly blond hair and blue eyes . . . just like the guy she had been with for the past several hours. Even if it wasn't Monty Whalen, the guy asleep out by the fireplace was still pretending to be Craig Dolan for some reason. That wasn't a good sign.

She bolted her door and returned to bed, but her earlier

sleepiness was long gone. She reviewed the events since this morning. First of all, the new officer was on the trail four days earlier than he was due to start his position. Why would he be there instead of at least coming to the Stephenville office to introduce himself first? And how could he possibly write his final exam in Stephenville in the morning when he was spending the night on Widow's Peak? When he went outside to gather firewood, she had spied him through the window scanning the outside area in a very tense fashion, as though he feared being observed. Then, when the radio broadcast was announced about the manhunt for Monty Whalen, he turned off the radio. When she objected to this, he grew defensive.

Melanie lay on the bed, waiting for sounds of movement from the next room. He was said to be armed and dangerous. Would he come bursting into her bedroom with a pistol aimed at her? Whenever she became nervous, her bladder worked overtime, and now she really felt the need to go to the washroom. She held it in for what seemed like hours, until she could manage it no longer.

She unlatched the door and opened it as quietly as possible. The fireplace cast a glow on the young man's face; his eyes were closed and his breathing even. She quietly moved past him and slipped into the bathroom.

When she returned, she was struck by how peaceful the young man looked when he was asleep. His stern look was gone, and he looked so innocent, like the man she started to get to know earlier that evening. She then remembered another part of the broadcast that said the escapee had a cross tattooed behind his left ear. Melanie leaned over his sleeping form and gently pulled back the hair behind his left ear. She jumped. The guy on the couch *was* Monty Whalen!

She turned, but before she could move away, his arm shot up. He grabbed her wrist and sprang from the couch.

"Did you find what you were looking for?" he hissed.

Melanie's lips quivered in fear, and she was unable to utter a word. She stood motionless under his intense scrutiny.

"I'm sure you saw the tattoo you were looking for. Now you know who I am."

"Yes, I d-do," she stammered uneasily. "You're Craig Dolan."

"Don't play stupid, Melanie. You know I'm Monty Whalen . . . killer at large."

"You're not going to hurt me, are you?" Melanie pleaded.

"Not if you don't give me reason, but you must realize that I can't let you leave until I'm safely away from here in the morning. Until then, I have to make sure that you won't run."

He found a thick length of cord in the closet and bound Melanie's hands behind her back. She knew it was useless to resist, as he was much larger than she. Even if she were able to run, he was armed and dangerous and would likely shoot her in the back.

AT HEART

For the remainder of the night, neither of them slept. They just sat on the sofa and talked. Monty left the station once during the night, securing the other end of Melanie's rope to a metal hook on the wall. She managed to lean over just far enough to see him through the window. She wondered why he had walked to the edge of Widow's Peak with a long bundle of coiled rope. He was crouched down low with his back to her, so she couldn't see what he was doing. She only hoped he was not planning to throw her from the ledge.

When he returned, he released her tether from the wall and even loosened her wrist bonds. He apologized for tying them so tightly, and Melanie thought it odd that someone accused of murder and declared armed and dangerous would be so gentle.

They finished the bottle of brandy in the early hours of the morning, and Melanie decided she would ask her captor to tell her his story.

Monty Whelan had been taken from his biological parents when he was two years of age and placed in the Mount Cashel orphanage in St. John's. His parents had been charged with neglect and he had never seen them again. He only wished that the Christian Brothers had neglected him as well, but, unfortunately, that was not to be. Over the next ten years he suffered verbal, physical, and sexual abuse from several Brothers at the home. The only light in his otherwise dismal world was the constant companionship of his half-brother, Craig Dolan, who was also a resident of the orphanage.

Craig was three years Monty's senior and had been removed from his home a year before Monty's birth. Although the boys shared the same mother, they had different fathers, and the lack of love and attention they received from their mother and respective fathers was very similar. The boys bonded, and they vowed they would always stick together. However, they were helpless to protect each other from the Christian Brothers. If one intervened on the other's behalf, they would both receive the same punishment.

They had managed to escape several times, but they were always found and dragged back to the orphanage, where they would be subjected to severe beatings until the Brothers felt the boys had learned their lesson. Once, they even made it to the police, but their allegations against the Christian Brothers fell on deaf ears, and they were escorted back to face another onslaught of punishment. During the last five years of Monty's life at the orphanage, he suffered the severe beatings alone, after Craig had been adopted by a couple in Stephenville.

When Monty turned twelve, Mount Cashel closed its doors permanently and over the next four years he was sent from one dysfunctional foster home to another. He had a difficult time adjusting to each new residence and was thought to be a "problem child." He was often subjected to more physical violence in his various residences, but as he grew older, he grew tougher and started to fight back. This promptly led him to a new family.

Monty thought his life had finally taken a turn for the better when he turned sixteen and moved to Stephenville to live with Jessie and Harold Ellsworth, only three houses down the road from Craig. Jessie was a short, stocky woman with crimson cheeks and the heart of an angel. In Monty's eyes she was a saint who never had a negative word to say about anyone. Harold was a tall, hefty ex-military man who ran his home like a command post, and he ruled with an iron fist. This didn't bother Monty much, as he spent most of his waking hours away from home, hanging out with Craig.

Initially, Monty's only problem in the Ellsworth home was the amount of liquor Harold consumed. When he drank, he became quite obnoxious and wounded Jessie with his serpent's tongue. This hurt Monty more than the beatings he had endured over the years. Jessie was the closest he had ever come to having a real mother, and he did not want her harmed in any way. However, he held his tongue during Harold's drunken tirades, because he thought it would make the situation worse for Jessie if he interfered. Also, he was afraid he would be forced to leave. He didn't want to be evicted from the only place he had ever considered home.

LISA IVANY and ROBERT HUNT

Things were going well at the Ellsworth residence until yesterday, when Monty came home early from his job at a local restaurant and witnessed Harold striking his wife repeatedly. His verbal attacks were one thing, but Monty would not stand by and watch this physical assault.

He lunged at Harold, knocking him back against the wall before he could strike Jessie again. Monty quickly pulled a Swiss Army knife from his pocket and held it against the older man's throat. At first, Harold seemed a little disoriented from the surprise attack. However, he quickly retaliated with renewed strength and shoved Monty, toppling him backward over a kitchen stool. Before Monty recovered from the attack, Harold had seized the weapon out of his foster son's hand and raised it with the intent of plunging it into the boy.

Before the knife could descend and hit its target, Harold's arm was grabbed from behind by Jessie. She was openly sobbing and begging him to leave the boy alone, but he ignored her pleas. When he turned to settle the score with Monty, who was just starting to rise from the floor, Jessie jumped in front of her husband. He had raised the weapon and it was thrusting downward, and it caught Jessie in the upper left chest, dropping her instantly to the floor.

Monty ran to Jessie and cradled her in his lap. He yelled at Harold, "Call an ambulance!" as he placed pressure against the wound to staunch the flow of blood, but it was to no avail. Within seconds, Jessie drew her last shaky breath.

AT HEART

Harold cried, "Jessie, oh my God! She's dead, she's dead!" He pushed Monty away from his wife, screaming, "This is your fault. You've been nothing but trouble since you came into this house, and now you've killed my wife!"

"No, I didn't. You were the one with the knife and you were the one who stabbed her! You're an animal and I hope you rot in jail!" Monty screamed.

"You're the one who is going to jail, boy, especially when I tell the police you did it."

Realizing that the old man would deliberately frame him for Jessie's death, Monty felt his only recourse was to flee and get as far away from Stephenville as possible. With a history of being a troublemaker who had been juggled from one foster home to the other, he was sure he would not get a break from the law.

When Monty had relayed the night's events to his brother, Craig suggested Widow's Peak as a safe refuge until they could plan their next move. By Monday, Craig should have enough money and supplies gathered to get him out of the province, at least until the truth came out. The boys knew that Harold would slip up during one of his drunken bouts and reveal what he had done. Until then, Monty could not return home.

Monty finished his narrative and saw tears in Melanie's eyes. She sat in silence, and he wondered if she sympathized with his plight or whether she even believed him at all. He knew how easily people were swayed by the media. It didn't matter if a person was innocent or guilty, as long as there was sensationalism. People listening to the broadcasts about him would have him tried and convicted in their minds.

Breaking the silence, Melanie whispered, "You've really had a rough life, haven't you?"

"Yeah, you could say that. Does that mean you believe me?"

"Yes I do."

"Then I guess I can trust you not to run if I untie the rope," Monty said as he pulled her forward on the couch to release her bindings.

He flinched when she embraced him with a tender hug, but he relaxed moments later when he realized she was not letting go. Suddenly, tears began to flow down his cheeks. He cried for the loss of his childhood innocence, for the failure of the justice system to protect him, but mostly he cried for the loss of a mother's love.

Monty fell asleep, nestled next to Melanie, after trying all night to convince her that he could not turn himself in and plead his case. He knew he would not get a fair trial, especially with Harold setting him up. The law had failed him when he was continually being molested by the Brothers at the orphanage, and they failed him every time they placed him with another dysfunctional family where he was either abused or neglected. No, he knew his only chance of survival was to run as long and as far as he could.

AT HEART

By morning, just before they drifted off to sleep, Melanie was convinced of this as well.

"Monty Whalen, this is Constable Chatman of the Royal Canadian Mounted Police!" the bullhorn announced in the quiet morning air. "Come out with your hands in the air and no one will get hurt."

Melanie and Monty jumped from the couch, now very much awake. They crouched low and crawled to a window. They counted four RCMP officers spread out along the front perimeter of the station, and Melanie saw Drew near the side window.

Monty escaped through the rear door, walking backward with his arm wrapped around Melanie's neck and a sharp knife levelled at her jugular. He hauled her over the muddy terrain, gradually backing up to the edge of the cliff.

"Back off or I'll slit her throat!" he yelled.

"There's no need for anyone to get hurt," Constable Chatman stated. "Let the woman go and we can all walk out of here."

"Yeah, and I walk right into a jail cell, right?"

"No. We just want to talk to you, that's all."

"Forget it. I'm through talking to the cops. Now, I told you to back off or she dies!"

The police officers did as he asked, and Drew also reluctantly slipped farther from the woman he loved. When they were a safe distance away, Monty reached down and brought up a rope, which he tied tightly around his waist.

He whispered in Melanie's ear, "Thanks for believing in me. I'll never forget you."

Monty placed his arm around her neck once again, but this time he hugged her. He then released his hold, backed up a few steps, and jumped over the edge of the cliff.

Melanie spun around, but he was gone. She looked over the edge and saw his quick descent down the steep valley with the rope he had secured the night before. When he neared the end of the rope, he swung to a ledge and safety. Melanie then took the knife he had left at her feet and sliced the rope from its top moorings before the officers arrived at her side. By that time, the rope had disappeared and Monty had made it to a clump of dogberry trees, where he remained concealed.

"Are you okay?" Drew asked as he held Melanie.

"Yes, I'm fine."

"I was so worried when I saw how close he had you to the edge," he moaned. "Promise me you will never come up here with strange men again."

"I promise," she agreed. Chuckling, she said, "Does that mean I can't come up here with you?"

Before he could respond, they were surrounded by police officers who now stretched along the ledge. All eyes were fixed on the valley below, searching for the spot where Monty would have landed, but there was no sign of him.

"No one has ever survived a fall from Widow's Peak, so I

assume he didn't make it," Constable Chatman stated. "We'll head down to the east end of Buffer's Pass and start searching for the body."

When the officers and Drew had loaded up their gear in the station, Melanie excused herself to retrieve a glove she had dropped at the ledge. She found it next to the cut rope on the ground and raised it to her left cheek while facing Monty's sanctuary. She knew he was watching her. This was their pre-arranged signal for Melanie to let him know which direction to take . . . one that would take him in the opposite direction of the RCMP search party. If she touched her right cheek, Monty would go west, and if she touched her left cheek, he would go east. However, Melanie deliberately sent Monty toward the officers.

Although burdened with guilt at betraying her new friend, Melanie knew she was doing the right thing for him. He would probably hate her when he realized she had set him up, but hopefully he would learn to forgive her in time. She couldn't bear to see him spend the rest of his life as a fugitive from justice when he was actually the biggest victim of all. She felt that, once he had a chance to tell his side of the story, an intensive investigation would begin, putting pressure on his stepfather. After a few interrogations, Harold would surely make a mistake and incriminate himself. Then Monty would be free at last.

Steel Mountain

ROBERT HUNT

Abe Turner didn't know how long he had been laying semi-conscious on the ground. As he touched his hand to his forehead and felt a small trickle of blood from cuts above his right eye, his guess was he had been down for about ten minutes. He scanned the spot where he had fallen and the smoky mist that surrounded the area. Dizziness started to overtake him and he fought to stay awake. When he came to his senses, he checked himself for any further injuries. Aside from a number of small cuts on his face, the worst he could tell was a cracked rib.

He rolled over and pushed himself to a kneeling position before getting to his feet. As he stood up, he realized his side was worse than he'd thought, and his head began throbbing painfully.

AT HEART

"You've realy done it this time," he said to himself while massaging his injury. He sat on a large rock and went over the events of that day.

Seven-year-old Scott Williams had wandered away from home in Pasadena early that morning. He had been last seen in the Steel Mountain area with friends hiking some of the trails, but failed to return later that evening with the other children. They told his parents that Scott wanted to hike on his own. Abe, an old family friend, was the first person the boy's parents called. He knew the area very well. Now, in his haste to find the boy, he had slipped and fallen down a ravine and injured himself. Against his wife's wishes, he had gone ahead by himself before search parties could be formed. He realized now that he should have waited; he knew the terrain and figured he would have found him by now.

After resting for ten minutes, Abe got up and moved as fast as his cracked rib would allow. He manoeuvred through the heavy brush and, after a time, came out the other end of the base of the crevice. As he inched his way toward an incline and to freedom, a marten scurried down a small winding path ahead of him. He stopped, and thought he heard a distant shout. He listened a little longer, but all that came back to him was the wind blowing through the brush and the rustle of small creatures running among the trees.

Abe travelled the base of the cliff for another few moments, then looked up and spotted a good place for him to reach higher ground. He checked his rope and looped it into a sailor's knot, then secured it in place for his upward climb. He took a moment to catch his breath, knowing that the pain of pulling himself up the forty or fifty feet to safety would be a difficult chore. While leaning back against the rock facing, he listened to the wind ricochet off the rock formation and fall to the earth. Then he heard it again. It seemed to be a voice calling from far off in the distance. He held his breath. Again, the same sound came to him, and this time he was sure it was a voice.

Abe unhooked his climbing gear and looped the rope around his chest and back. He wouldn't climb up until he found out where the noise was coming from. He circled the stone wall for another few minutes, and when he came to a group of trees at the edge of a small clearing, he stopped and listened. Sure enough, it was indeed a voice, and Abe was sure whose it was. He hurried to the other side of the mountain. When he emerged, he stood on a small ridge. Looking down, he saw where the voice was coming from. A hundred feet below him, on a grassy ledge, was young Scott Williams. From his vantage point, Abe could see that Scott was perilously close to the edge. At this altitude and with these high winds, he knew that Scott would not be able to hear him. He had to get lower. As he started his downward climb, his ribs told him it would be slow going. After descending a few moments, he noticed that Scott was dazed and disoriented. He shouted out to him, but it was in vain.

"Scott! Scott, can you hear me?"

AT HEART

The boy had probably collapsed from exhaustion. Abe decided he had no other choice but to propel himself to the ledge to rescue him. But would the ledge hold them both? The pain in his side told Abe that getting to the boy and taking him off the ledge would be a difficult task. He had to act quickly; now he could see that Scott was unconscious, and he feared the boy might roll over the ledge at any time and plummet to his death.

In a matter of minutes, he had secured a line and was propelling down the mountain face toward the ledge. When he landed, he heard the outcropping crack as he laid his weight on it. He pushed himself back and hugged the cliff. He shouted to Scott, who looked back at Abe with dazed eyes.

Thinking fast as the ledge started to crumble, Abe grasped the rope tightly, braced himself on the soft ledge, reached out and grabbed Scott by his belt. Just as his fingers closed around the boy's belt, the ledge gave way and fell to the water a hundred feet below.

Abe looped a harness around Scott and started to move down the face of the rock. The boy was barely conscious, but he could see no sign of physical injury beyond a few minor bruises. Abe looked around and figured that it was better for them to go down here, rather than up. They could walk along the shoreline and hopefully climb up somewhere less hazardous. He prepared the rope to propel them both to the shore. Within minutes, he had himself and Scott dropping toward the water below.

Abe laid Scott down and examined him for any injuries. Shortly, Scott opened his eyes. He hugged Abe tightly and told him that he was walking along the edge of the trail and fell to the ledge below. Abe figured the worst was over, and that all they had to do was walk around the base of the mountain a ways and walk up a hundred-foot incline to safety. Realizing that Scott was more scared than hurt, he helped the boy to his feet and they both set off along the foothills.

It was starting to get dark as they reached a small beach. They went about fifty feet through some brush, when Abe was startled by a roar. Standing in front of them, blocking their path, was the biggest lynx Abe had ever seen. He quietly pushed Scott behind him as his mind raced to figure out what his next course of action should be.

Without turning his head, he said in a low voice, "Scott, whatever you do, don't move. If you do, it could startle him and he will probably attack. Be as still as you can."

However, the lynx began to growl and took a few confident steps toward the pair. Abe put his hand in his pocket and retrieved his folded pocket knife. Then he remembered that he was carrying search flares in his backpack. He slowly bent down, took one out, and waited for the lynx to get closer. When it was about ten feet away, Abe opened the flare and pushed it toward the animal. An orange and yellow flame shot out of the tube. The heat was tremendous, and the great cat howled and backed away. It seemed to reconsider its options, then shrank back into the brush, casting one last baleful glare at Abe and Scott before disappearing. Abe breathed a sigh of relief and Scott hugged his waist.

"Its okay, son," Abe said. "He's gone now and the worst is over. We'll be out of here soon."

"Okay, Mr. Turner. I'm all right as long as you're here."

Realizing he still had two other flares, Abe reached into his backpack and extracted his flare gun, loaded it, and he and Scott walked to the highest point of the hill as darkness started to descend on them. Abe got some firewood together and lit a fire to warm them. When he finished, he walked to an opening and shot the flare gun into the night air.

In half an hour, they were greeted by the welcome shouts of the search party. Abe lay down while a paramedic took a look at his injured rib.

When they were both ready to be carried out of Steel Mountain on stretchers, Scott turned to Abe and said, "Thanks for helping me, Mr. Turner. It will be a long time before I wander off by myself into the mountains again."

"You and me both, Scott," Abe said with a grin. "You and me both."

Lucky's Landing

LISA IVANY

Till death do us part. Lucky Canning obsessed over the wedding vows she exchanged with Morgan less than two years ago, on July 14. They were both thirty-one years of age and thought they had their whole lives ahead of them. Never did Lucky think she would be a widow by thirty-two.

She reflexively wiped away the tears sliding beneath her sunglasses while keeping one hand on the wheel of her red Toyota Corolla. Traffic was heavy on the Trans-Canada Highway, being Friday evening of the Victoria Day weekend. Newfoundlanders are avid campers, and regardless of weather conditions, every available campsite on the island would be occupied for the start of camping season. Last year at this time, she and Morgan were among the throng of camping enthusiasts.

Four hours after leaving her home in Mount Pearl,

AT HEART

Lucky arrived at Butt's Pond East. So far, the directions were easy enough to follow. Once she saw Square Pond Park to her left, she slowed down to make a right turn onto the first gravel road. She glanced once more at her map and continued on to Ken Cook cul-de-sac. The third road on the left, down over the hill, another left, and halfway down the road was the cottage she sought.

She was looking forward to her three-day weekend of solitude to relax, read a good book, and get away from her family. Although they meant well and were trying their best to help her deal with her grief, they also smothered her at times. Thanks to the generosity of her friends, Melvin and Grace Wicks, who offered the use of their cottage at Butt's Pond, she had a temporary reprieve. It was just what she needed.

Ring. Lucky pulled into the circular driveway of Wicks' Manor just as her cellphone announced an incoming call.

"Hello."

"Hi, Lucky," Melvin said. "Just checking to see if you've arrived at the cottage yet."

"Actually, I've just landed," she replied.

"That's good. Remember, if you need anything, I'm just a call away, and the neighbours around you are always willing to lend a hand. Brian Shugarue is next door to you, and Aubrey Goodyear is down the road at number sixty."

"Thanks, Melv. I'll keep that in mind, but I'm sure I'll be okay here at your place," she stated. "You and Grace have no idea how much this retreat means to me."

"Just enjoy your stay. That's all that matters to us," he answered. "Talk to you later."

"Goodbye, Melv." Lucky smiled at Melvin's concern.

The cottage was a grey, two-storey structure with a white patio along the front and left side. It was bordered on three sides by trees with trails leading off to nearby cottages. The neighbours were close enough to offer a sense of security yet far enough away to allow privacy.

She cut the car's engine and removed her dust-covered sunglasses and cap, realizing the error in leaving the window down while driving on the dry dirt road. She stood and brushed her fingers through her short auburn hair where the cap had flattened it. Morgan had loved her long, curly locks, and she had only recently summoned the courage to cut them. She wondered what Morgan would say if he saw her short hairdo. She wished with all her heart that he *could* see her. Only then, she thought, could she come back to the land of the living.

Lucky remembered the last time she saw Morgan, before he sailed away aboard the *Camilla*, a freight ship headed for Norway. It was July 28 of last year, just a couple of weeks after their first anniversary. He had placed a lingering kiss on her lips before heading up the gangway and onto the deck. As the ship pulled away from the St. John's dockyard, he stood at the railing, waving and blowing soft, feathery kisses in the air to her. He was one of the crewmen on board, but his shift in the engine room didn't start until the next morning, so he stayed up on deck wishing his wife a fond farewell until he and the ship were out of sight. He stood tall in his faded denim jeans and the long-sleeved white shirt that accentuated his sun-bronzed skin. Lucky remembered how strikingly handsome he looked, leaning against the rail with the brisk wind whipping through his thick black hair as he sailed away.

Several days later, the *Camilla* was discovered foundering at sea with no occupants aboard. Most of the crew members made it to the safety of the lifeboats and were later rescued, but many men had perished in the icy waters of the Atlantic. Several bodies were never found, and Morgan was one of the missing. From the captain's account, they were fighting an angry storm when a thunderous blast from below deck rocked the ship. Thick billows of charcoal smoke rolled up from the engine room, chased by wicked orange flames. The fire itself claimed some lives, while the seething ocean gorged itself on the sailors who were unfortunate enough to be swept off the ship.

"Hi there," a voice called, interrupting Lucky's thoughts.

She looked in the direction of the voice to the man next door and thought she was seeing a ghost. His tall stature, dark hair, and rugged features were enough like Morgan's to deem him her late husband's twin. Even the way he was grinning at her, with the slight curl of his upper left lip, was identical to Morgan's smile.

Composing herself, Lucky replied, "Hi. You must be Brian."

"Actually, I'm Dave Lannigan. Brian's away for the weekend and offered me his cottage."

"There's a lot of that going around. I have this place on loan from Melvin and Grace for the weekend. I'm Lucky."

"Yes, you *are* lucky. That's a beautiful cottage they have there. I was in it with Brian last summer."

"No," she laughed. "I meant my name is Lucky. I'm Lucky Canning."

"That's a cute name," he said, laughing.

"Well, I have to get unpacked. It was nice meeting you."

"You too. I'm sure I'll see you later."

Lucky was still smiling as she unpacked her groceries for the weekend, and it was a strange feeling. She couldn't remember the last time she had laughed or even smiled with any real sense of sincerity. *How can I smile when my heart is breaking?* she thought. However, she had to admit to herself that it felt good. *Maybe it's because he looks so much like Morgan*, she rationalized. Once she had justified her breach of solemnity, her conscience was appeased.

That evening, after several failed attempts to light the barbecue, Lucky kicked it in frustration.

"I don't think that's going to get it started," Dave yelled from next door.

"Well, nothing else seems to be working."

"It's probably out of propane. Why don't you bring your

steak over and join me for dinner?" Dave offered. "I've just lit the grill, and I didn't even have to kick it," he teased.

"Sounds good," Lucky said. "I'll be over in a few minutes."

She raced to the bedroom and grabbed her makeup. When she looked at herself in the mirror, she realized she had a lot of work ahead of her. With lightning speed, she applied mascara, eyeshadow, and a fresh splash of lip gloss. There was no time to tame her frizzy locks. She quickly lathered a small amount of gel through her fingers and applied it to her hair until she had a sleek wet look, much to her liking.

Satisfied that she looked presentable, Lucky strolled to the cottage next door. The evening sun provided enough warmth to allow the diners to eat outside on the patio and enough of a breeze to keep the mosquitos at bay. Lucky already knew it would be hard to tear herself away from this serene atmosphere when the weekend ended.

As they sipped wine on the wicker sofa and exchanged information about themselves, they found they had a lot in common. Lucky couldn't help noticing how similar Dave's mannerisms were to Morgan's. She felt drawn to him and found herself revealing her life story.

"Let's go for a walk," Dave suggested.

"Yes, let's," she agreed. "I wouldn't mind walking off some of that dinner."

"Yeah, you did seem to take quite a fancy to the scalloped potatoes."

"Are you saying I ate too much?" Lucky huffed.

"No," he grinned. "I think it's great that you're keeping the potato farmers in business."

Dave sped past her before she could jab him in the arm. He was still laughing after she took chase, finally catching up with him at the end of the path.

They strolled down the road, admiring the rustic cabins and the modern cottages along the way. To a casual observer, they looked the picture of two young lovers as they walked along, in no particular hurry to reach their destination. A "For Sale" sign was attached to a post by the driveway of 34 Tulken Lane, and they went in for a closer inspection.

A huge birch tree rose from the centre of the drive, its bounty of branches laden with buds awaiting the summer sun to blossom. Beyond the tree, they walked up the front steps of the cabin onto a large covered deck. It was a shade of walnut brown trimmed with white, and the patio was sheltered by a roof housing four skylights. Lucky fell in love with the place without even setting foot inside the door. She knew she would be the owner by the end of the weekend.

"I'm going to buy this place," she blurted out.

"Are you serious?" Dave asked incredulously.

"Yes, I'm positive," Lucky replied. "I even know what I'm going to name it."

"What's that?"

"Lucky's Landing."

It was twilight by the time they headed back. Without street lights, the trek was a little difficult and Lucky felt spooked. Dave, sensing her unease, held her hand until they were safely on her doorstep.

"I had a lovely time tonight," she said. "Thanks for cooking dinner."

"The pleasure was all mine."

"I guess I better get inside. Good night."

"Good night, Lucky."

He slowly moved his head down to hers with the intention of kissing her good night, but she sidestepped him and went inside. She leaned against the inside of the door, trying to catch her breath while her heart danced in a frenzied rhythm. She felt like she had just betrayed Morgan.

Before noon the following day, Lucky had met with the owner and made on offer on the cabin at 34 Tulken Lane. The money she received from Morgan's life insurance policy was more than enough to cover the cost, and she knew he would approve. The dwelling itself needed a lot of attention, but she could see definite potential. It consisted of a kitchen, bathroom, living room, and two bedrooms. Everything inside was white, but she knew a visit to the nearest paint shop would remedy that.

Not one to procrastinate, Lucky got everything she needed for painting while the sun was still shining directly overhead. When she had asked Dave where the closest hardware store was, instead of giving her directions, he drove her there himself. They boarded his pickup and within ten minutes arrived at Pritchett's Building Supplies in Gambo, the nearest community to the pond. Armed with paint cans, brushes, rollers, and other painting paraphernalia, they loaded up the truck.

A soft shade of putty covered the walls of both the living room and kitchen, while the bathroom was painted with pale lilac and the guest room was a gentle tone of mint green. For her own bedroom, she had chosen a celestial yellow in an effort to re-energize and renew her spirit. Whether it would work was yet to be seen. However, new life had been breathed into the place with a few coats of paint and Lucky was quite happy with the result. Lucky and Dave worked tirelessly for the remainder of the weekend, and by the time Lucky returned home to Mount Pearl, the painting was finished.

By the end of June, Lucky was approved for a four-month leave of absence from her job as assistant manager of the Battery Hotel. She enjoyed the perks of her new position, such as getting time off when she needed it. Just a year ago, she was still working as a receptionist at the front desk, and getting leave for even two weeks was difficult.

She packed what belongings she could squeeze into the car and moved to her summer home at Butt's Pond. Indeed, after a lot of work, it now looked more like a cottage than a cabin. She knew she could never have done it on her own, and she owed her new community of neighbours at Butt's Pond a huge debt of gratitude, especially Melvin and Dave. Certainly Dave had become a neighbour, staying at the Pond for the remainder of the summer to help her with the renovations. His job as an English teacher afforded him this enviable privilege.

On the occasions when Dave wasn't around, Lucky was well looked after by her new friends. They trained her in the ways of cabin dwelling, realizing her ineptitude early on. Harvey and Mary Pike across the road extinguished the fire she started in her kerosene lantern and kept an eye on her during thunderstorms after learning of her sheer terror of them. When her water pipes broke and her kitchen flooded, Tom and Ann Starkes next door came over immediately and fixed the problem. Yes, Lucky was indeed happy with her new community at the Pond.

Dave was a frequent visitor to Lucky's Landing, and although he wanted more than friendship with Lucky, she could not persuade her heart to let go of the past. At times she would nearly let down her guard when he would do or say something quite typical of Morgan. However, she knew he was not Morgan, and she was not willing to settle for less.

"Hey, pretty lady!" Dave called as he sprinted up the front steps.

"Hey, yourself," Lucky replied.

"Do you have any plans for lunch?"

"Not really," she answered. "I'll probably put something on the barbecue. It's too hot to cook inside today."

"How about a picnic?"

"Sounds good. Let me see what I can throw together."

"It's already taken care of. I have a feast prepared in the basket, waiting in the car," he replied. "You just need your sunglasses and bathing suit. I thought we'd drive over to the other side of the pond, go for a dip in the water, and have lunch."

"Sounds great to me."

"Maybe you should put on a hat so you don't get sunstroke in this heat."

"Yes, Dad," she teased.

Since it was Tuesday and most people were working, the beach was nearly deserted. They strolled barefoot through the sand, until they found a quiet alcove, and spread out their blanket and picnic gear. While Dave retrieved sodas from the cooler, Lucky opened the basket to see what he had brought to eat. She was surprised to see salads, fried chicken, bread, cheese, fruit, and nuts.

"Wow!" she exclaimed. "You've brought enough to feed an Army!"

"I wanted to make sure you had everything your heart desires," he laughed.

There was that warm and generous smile of his again. Only this time, the expression didn't look like Morgan anymore, but rather like Dave himself. *I wonder why*, she thought. From the moment she met Dave, he had reminded her of Morgan in his looks and actions. However, lately she was thinking about him as a separate person and someone she truly liked. *Does this mean Morgan is fading from my mind?* she thought with a sudden attack of conscience.

They swam in the pond's warm water, raced back to their towels, and feasted on lunch. Afterwards, they strolled hand in hand along the beach, where the water caressed the sand and tickled their toes. Lucky was amazed at the euphoria she felt. Whether it was due to the serenity of the deserted beach, the perfect summer day, or the special man at her side, she knew she didn't want it to end.

Just before dusk, they returned to their blanket to pack up their things and leave. However, Dave surprised her by extracting a chocolate Amaretto cheesecake from the cooler. Lucky's expression was one of astonishment.

"This is my absolute favourite dessert!" she exclaimed. "I didn't know you could buy these around here."

"I didn't buy it," he retorted. "I'll have you know I made it myself."

"You are a man of many hidden talents," she said as she tasted the delicacy. "This tastes as heavenly as the ones from the Battery Hotel that Morgan used to buy me."

A look of sadness crossed Lucky's face at this revelation, and Dave felt he was losing ground to a ghost once again. He wondered if the day would ever come when Morgan Canning would no longer be a wedge between them.

Lucky saw the change in Dave's demeanour at the mention of her late husband and realized that he had misinterpreted her expression. Her sorrow was not at the thought of Morgan, but in hurting Dave by her faux pas. She wanted to grab the words and swallow them as soon as they passed her lips, but it was too late.

"I'm sorry," she whispered. "I won't mention his name again."

"No, Lucky. That wouldn't be fair to you . . . or to us. I don't want you to feel you have to hide anything from me."

"But . . ." she started.

"No buts," he interrupted. "Finish your dessert while I go for one last dip in the water."

She watched him swim back and forth with movements like a professional athlete. He sliced through the waves with ease and agility, and Lucky enjoyed the performance. She was only now realizing how much she had come to care for him and how much she had been hurting him with her lack of commitment.

She sat on the blanket with her notebook and pen and started to write as she watched the sun make its slow descent to the horizon. The soothing sound of the waves rushing to shore, intermingled with the call of a loon across the pond, inspired Lucky's poetic creativity.

She had just finished the first stanza of her poem. Droplets of water sprinkled Lucky as Dave collapsed beside her.

"Oohh! You're getting me wet, you beast!" she squealed in mock irritation.

"How about a hair shower," he laughed as he shook his head and doused her with droplets from his wet locks.

"You're getting my notebook wet, you fiend!" she giggled.

AT HEART

"Have you written anything?"

"Just one stanza so far. I guess the sunset inspired me to write a poem for you."

"For me?" he beamed. "I'd love to hear it."

"Okay, here goes," she replied.

"As I watch the sunset, fading slowly into night / your face consumes my memory even though you're not in sight / While quiet twilight deepens to the darkest shade of blue / I'm grateful for the things I love, and most especially for you."

Lucky allowed the final line in her poem to linger in the air for a moment, as though allowing its impact to penetrate her self-erected barriers. In her heart, she would always love Morgan, but she knew he would not want her to continue living in the past. She also knew she needed someone like Dave in her life to fill the empty void and to help her smile, not only on the outside, but on the inside as well.

Lucky's inhibitions vanished as she lay under the stars, entwined in the arms of the man she could no longer imagine a future without. He had inspired the words in her poem and she knew she was now ready to start living—and loving—again.

Sniper

ROBERT HUNT

Often, when Lloyd Snow closes his eyes, shadows of memory beckon him. He thinks back to July 7, 1997, and the actions of Master Sergeant Eric Ryan of Lourdes, Newfoundland, and Corporal Calvin "Whip" Buchanan of Des Moines, Iowa. They showed bravery that day, and a sacrifice was made for the men in their unit on a day that began like any other, but ended in tragedy on the war-torn streets of Sarajevo.

The scene plays over again in his mind, always moving toward the same conclusion. What if they could do it all over again? Would they have handled themselves differently? But the ending was always the same. Corporal Lloyd Snow was just one of many players in a drama that unfolded at breakneck speed.

* * *

AT HEART

We were called the PPCLI, or the Princess Patricia's Canadian Light Infantry. Our day started off with Sergeant Ryan, Corporal Jack Pardy, and I of the 25th Light Infantry Dragons, doing a sweep, or a check, of nearby Pangaluka. It was a small town with a population of 700 people nestled in the hills several miles from Sarajevo. Our company had done a preliminary surveillance of the town the day before, and nothing seemed out of the ordinary. Captain Clyde Raymond ordered the three of us and seventeen other men to check the area and report back to camp at 1500 hours.

We synchronized our watches at 1300 hours and began our patrol. Pangaluka had been "swept" yesterday because a firefight had broken out there. We were told it was safe. But this "Sunday stroll" turned out to be more than a walk in the park. We made our way to the outskirts of the city and began our three-mile walk through. Somehow, the feeling of being watched would not leave me. It never does on patrol. It stays with you until your patrol is finished, and with some, until their tour of duty is finished.

Street by street we continued, watching the small doors and windows for any sign of activity. The march-through was done in two three-by-five diamond formations, with the remainder of the men covering the rear. In silence, we marched along the rock and concrete streets, looking for any signs of danger for our follow-up squads, who had yet to enter the town. By 1410 hours we had canvassed the entire area, and there was nothing to report. All was quiet.

That is what we did. We were the guinea pigs who swept an area after every conflict to see if there were any lingering signs of the enemy. Of course, we took all the glory from the other men in the platoon. They knew the dangers we faced. And in this case, at 1423, our walk would be interrupted.

I was in the third column of three when I saw Private Bill Sweeney, thirty feet in front of me, plunge forward onto his knees and topple over. On instinct, we all hit the ground. The word "sniper" quickly made its way through the group as another man checked Sweeney and pulled him safely behind a brick compound. We scanned the area, but could see nothing.

Sergeant Ryan's voice rang out. "Where is he? Does anyone have a bead on him?"

A chorus of negatives echoed back from the men lying prone in the street.

"The way the shot hit Sweeney, Sergeant, I'd say it came from the building on our left," shouted Private Luke Connolly from behind an abandoned pickup.

"Okay, guys, heads up," Ryan ordered. "We all need to take cover behind that wall to our right. On the count of three, I want all of you to concentrate fire on that building. On my count. One . . . two . . . three."

As one, the men scrambled to their feet and bolted for the wall, while those who had reached the relative safety of the truck covered them by opening fire on the suspect building. I sprinted the twenty or so feet to the wall, and bullets ripped up the concrete at my feet. Private Art Tarrant was shot in the lower arm, but luckily he was the only one injured in the exchange. Within a few moments, the dust had settled and all was eerily silent.

"Whip!" Sergeant Ryan yelled. "Find this guy or we'll be pinned down here."

Calvin "Whip" Buchanan, our sharpshooter from Des Moines, nodded in Sergeant Ryan's direction and looked about for our invisible attacker.

"What do you see, Whip?" Ryan asked.

"I see there is not one, but at least a couple of snipers in that building, Sarge. Let me see if I can even up the odds a little bit."

A light breeze blew the dust and gravel along the cobblestone walkway where we lay in anticipation. The silence was split by shattering glass and the sound of exploding rounds as the second-storey window blew out, and an enemy soldier fell through the opening and plummeted to the ground thirty feet below. Another shot rang out, and a cry of pain sounded from the second floor of the building next door.

"Nice shooting, Whip," Sergeant Ryan said as he examined the windows. "Concentrate your weapons on the second floor, men, and let's see if we can smoke some of these guys out into the street."

The city block erupted with gunfire as both sides exchanged fire. Bullets hit the wall where we lay, and pieces of the building chipped off and rained down on the street. Then, after what seemed an eternity, the firing stopped as quickly as it had started. Silence hung like death as we waited. It was as if the world had stood still.

Something caught the corner of my eye. I squinted, at first not believing what I was seeing. About forty feet across the open clearing was a young child, clutching her small doll and walking directly into the no man's land separating us from our attackers. More shots rang out as the child cried for her mother. We looked up at the building. The enemy was shooting at her! They were not trying to hit the girl, but narrowly missing her on purpose. We could hear their laughter as they toyed with the child in the open street.

"They're using her to flush us out," Sergeant Ryan shouted. "I have seen this before; they use the children of their enemies as bait to get them out in the open."

We could only watch in horror as they sent shot after shot ricocheting behind and in front of the screeching girl. She was no more than seven years old, I guessed as her terrified screams echoed across the deserted streets. *What is she doing here, in the middle of a war?* I thought. *What kind of men are these? They have no respect for human life.*

Anger tore at me as I watched the scene unfold. Hatred at what was happening here ate at my heart. Sergeant Ryan took a deep breath, looked at me, and said, "Snow, when I give the word, I want you and Pardy to concentrate fire on that second floor. Give me as much firepower as you can.

Radio Hawke and Power and tell them to concentrate their fire on that building. Do it now!" he said as he looked in fury at what was happening.

I grabbed the radio and relayed Sergeant Ryan's request to Hawke and Power on the other side of the structure. In a matter of minutes, their rapid fire began to pelt the building. Glass and the window framework shattered as rounds of gunfire eroded the side of the enemy compound. I turned my head in time to see Sergeant Ryan sprint from cover, hurtling the fifty yards toward the young child.

I watched the first bullet hit him in the leg. Blood spurted from the wound onto the pavement. He dropped, and I thought he was down, but he sprang up and fired directly at the building from a revolver that appeared in his hand. He was up again, and running toward the child. A second bullet ripped into his side, but this didn't slow him.

A third shot caught him in the shoulder. He lunged the remaining few feet and drew the crying girl into his protective arms. Angling his body to be used as a shield, he crawled atop the child. Bullets tore into his back. I watched, horrified, as his movements ceased. Then he looked at me and nodded, and I knew that he was playing possum. Of course! He was wearing his flak jacket!

"Whip, can you see the other two?" Sergeant Ryan shouted as a few rounds chipped pieces of stone around him.

As quickly as the words left his mouth, another enemy solider toppled out of the window and plunged to his death.

Sure enough, Whip had located another sniper. The sharpshooter scanned the building again with his rifle's telescopic sight. He signalled that, as near as he could tell, only one enemy sniper remained.

No movement from the building now. I figured the sniper had moved to another location somewhere inside . . . or that the enemy was playing possum, too.

"Hawke," Whip shouted, "I want you to cover me. I'm going in to find our friend. Any sign of him, or if you get a clear shot, take him out."

Hawke trained his sights on the building, then fired repeatedly to cover Whip as he darted across the open area of the compound. The sniper slowly inched to the opposite side of the building, found an open window, and crawled through.

Moments passed. We waited at the ready, tensing as we heard several shots from inside the building. Then, slowly, Whip crawled to a blown-out window and shouted down to us. "Sergeant? I think I got the last one. But be careful, there may be more of them on other floors. I've been hit, but forget about me until it's safe to come in."

Several of us scrambled from our protective cover and made our way inside the building. We checked all the floors for hidden compartments, and, when we were certain the building was secure, we gave the okay for the others to come in.

We found Corporal Buchanan sitting against the wall on the second floor. We knew he was dead even before the medic checked his vitals. He had taken two of the sniper's bullets in the neck. We took off our helmets and offered a silent prayer for our fallen friend.

We went outside as the medic checked Sergeant Ryan and the small child. Ryan had taken several bullets in his leg, arm, and side, but none were of a serious nature. He knew by looking at our faces that Whip had not made it. He took off his helmet, looked at the building, and bowed his head in respect. Tears welled up in his eyes as he blessed himself.

Within minutes, scores of men were coming up behind us and treating my wounded friends. In the excitement, I didn't realize that I had been cut by glass when entering the building. A large wound extended across my arm and was bleeding profusely. A medic made me sit down, and he began to suture it. I surveyed the scene and marvelled at how peaceful this area had been about an hour ago. It was now silent again, but it was the silence of the dead.

Eight years later, as he looks back on those days he and his comrades had spent in peril, Corporal Lloyd Snow offers a salute to Sergeant Ryan and Whip Buchanan, two of the bravest men he had ever met. He smiles as he recalls a certain biblical passage, John 15:13, that stayed with him for many years after that day in Sarajevo. "Greater love hath no man than this, that a man lay down his life for his friends."

Ever After

LISA IVANY

Stacey Jarvis twirled one of her auburn curls around the pencil in her hand, a typical habit when she was frustrated. She stared at the blank screen of her laptop, trying to visualize the opening line of her next story. The deadline for submission to her publisher was Wednesday—just two days away—and she needed one more short story to complete her manuscript. After the overwhelming success of her first book of stories, her publisher urged her to do a follow-up volume. However, try as she might, she could not free her mind to concentrate on the task at hand. The only thoughts and images taking residence in her head were those of her last conversation with Dane Marin, the man who had stolen her heart and then casually ripped it apart.

He called her last evening to cancel their dinner plans,

even though she had toiled all day in the kitchen preparing his favourite dishes. When she inquired as to the reason, he was quite evasive, saying he just didn't want to give her the wrong impression by joining her for dinner too often. When Stacey insisted on knowing exactly what he meant, he said he wanted their relationship to remain platonic—it would interfere with their office dynamics if they became involved. Office dynamics! There had been an undeniable chemistry between them since he joined the staff at *Tebber Magazine* two months ago, and he had done nothing to discourage it. In fact, he had been sending strong signals her way. Stacey didn't like second-guessing people and, at thirty-five, she felt she was beyond the age of playing games.

How could he just lead me on like that? she fumed. He didn't even have the courage to speak to her face to face, but rather took the coward's way out by talking to her on the phone. She assumed he knew she was intelligent enough to know how lame his excuse was, so he must have feared a confrontation with her.

Dane's job required him to interview victims of crimes and natural disasters for his column. He had a keen ability to comfort those he spoke with. Stacey felt like a victim herself, but for some reason he had chosen not to comfort her.

A knock at the front door provided Stacey with a temporary reprieve from her writing task and, certainly, from her disturbing thoughts. She laid the computer to one side and jumped up from the recliner. When she opened the door, there stood Belle, her best friend and co-worker, holding two cups from Tim Hortons.

"Are you okay?" Belle asked.

"I will be once you come in and hand over that hot chocolate," she quipped.

"I'm serious, Stacey. When you didn't show up for work today, I asked Dane if you had been sick over the weekend, but he said he hadn't seen you since Friday. I knew you were planning a nice dinner for him yesterday, so I was worried."

"It's sweet of you to be so concerned about me, Belle, but I'm fine."

Stacey's red, swollen eyes betrayed her attempt at control, and she certainly could not fool her friend. When Belle squeezed her in a comforting hug, a torrent of fresh tears spilled from Stacey's eyes. One hour and many tissues later, she had revealed all the details from the heartbreaking phone call the evening before.

The two women put their heads together, but they could not figure out the sudden change in Dane's attitude. Although Stacey had only known him since he joined the magazine in March, their connection had been instantaneous and strong. She had been so certain that her feelings were being reciprocated, but now she was confused and felt like a fool.

"Well, I guess I know why he hasn't kissed me yet . . . and why he was so rigid when I hugged him good night on Friday," she said. "I thought he was just shy, but obviously he isn't attracted to me."

"I don't think that's the case at all," Belle countered. "You need to talk to him and find out the truth."

"I tried that last night, but he's sticking to the story that co-workers shouldn't date. I must look like such an idiot in his eyes."

"Don't sell yourself short. He's the loser here, and I'm sure he'll figure that out once he's had time to think it through."

"If he's the loser, then why am I the one with the broken heart?" Stacey sniffed.

"The bigger the heart, the harder it breaks, my friend," Belle said.

After a restless night, Stacey arose the next morning determined to hold her head high and return to work. She knew it would be difficult to avoid Dane, with merely a divider separating their cubicles, but she couldn't hide out in her apartment forever.

The wonderful world of cosmetics transformed Stacey's wan complexion into a healthy glow. Soft rose blush accentuated her well-defined cheekbones, and her tired sapphire eyes sparkled between long black lashes. She assessed her reflection in the mirror and was pleased to see that, although she felt like hell on the inside, she looked great on the outside. *At least Dane won't see how much he's hurt me*, she thought. She was determined not to let him have that satisfaction.

She arrived early, bypassed his empty cubicle, and

slipped behind her own desk to get to work, answering letters for her advice column. Work was what she needed to keep her mind distracted, even if it involved advising other people on how to deal with their love problems.

"Good Morning, Stacey," a voice called from across the aisle.

"Morning, Jeremy."

"What's wrong?" Jeremy asked softly as he popped his lanky frame into her doorway.

"Nothing's wrong."

"I can tell by the tone of your voice that something's up. Come on, Stacey, spill it."

"I just didn't sleep well last night, that's all."

"All right, I'll accept that for now. Don't forget this is wing night."

"Sorry, Jeremy, but I have to bow out tonight. My manuscript is due tomorrow, so I have to finish it tonight."

"You have to eat dinner anyway, so why don't you work at your manuscript after work and then join us at Darby's around 7:00? You can leave early if your story isn't finished."

"I'll try."

It had become a tradition for Stacey to meet with Jeremy, Ronnie, and Belle for wings at Darby's Pub every Tuesday night for the past year. Dane had also been joining them recently, and she wondered if he would show tonight.

Jeremy and Ronnie were a gay couple who worked together closely at the magazine, and they had no problem with the office dynamics of dating a co-worker. Stacey wanted to throw that up in Dane's face when she had the chance. *Let's see him refute that*, she thought. However, the opportunity didn't arise, because when Dane came to work, he was his usual charming self. He spoke to her several times throughout the day as though nothing had happened. *The jerk!* she thought. She played along with his stupid game and never let on that she was hurting. *I won't give him that much power over me*, she vowed to herself with stubborn pride.

Checking through her emails at the end of the day, she saw one from Carol Fewer, her publisher. The note read, *Stacey, I will be out of town on business until Monday. I've extended your submission deadline until then. Good luck with the manuscript.*

It was just what she needed, considering her state of mind. Since Dane had blown her off, she wasn't in the proper emotional state to write anything, especially for a manuscript comprised of romance stories. The title she had chosen was "Ever After," to tie in with the endings of her stories where the heroine always ended up with Mr. Right and they lived happily ever after. For a short time, she had hoped her own life was headed in that direction, but she realized her life was not a book of fiction, but rather a cold, hard dose of reality.

Stacey felt a mixture of both relief and disappointment at Darby's that evening when Dane failed to appear. As much as her head told her to move on, her heart was reminding her that she was still crazy about him. Wanting to drown her sorrows, she agreed to check out the new club, Jingles, with her friends when they finished their wings. Once she told them the deadline for her manuscript had been extended, they wouldn't have let her refuse anyway.

Vibrations coursed through their bodies before they even heard the music upon entering the nightclub. By the time they reached the end of the long entrance, the music prohibited normal speaking and they almost had to yell to be heard. Along the wall on the right was the bar, to the left was the bandstand, and a large area in the centre served as the dance floor.

"Why don't you get us a table while I get the drinks," Ronnie suggested.

"Sounds good to me," Jeremy replied. "Just don't go flirting with the bartender."

Stacey and Belle chuckled, because they had seen the obviously gay bartender. When they were seated, the girls scanned the room and noticed something odd. It wasn't obvious when they looked in the direction of the bar, but once they saw what was happening on the dance floor, their mouths dropped.

"Oh my God!" Stacey exclaimed. "Jeremy, you've brought us to a gay bar!"

"Yeah, what's wrong with that?"

"Well," she stammered.

"Make way for the drinks," Ronnie said as he rejoined them. "From the looks on your faces, girls, I assume you're enjoying the atmosphere," he laughed.

"I'm not sure about that yet," Belle answered.

"It's just that this is the first time we've been in a gay bar," Stacey explained.

Once the girls realized there was nothing unusual about the bar except for the fact that men were dancing with men, they settled down and relaxed. With the playful antics of her friends to entertain her, Stacey's problems were put on hold.

At the start of a slow song, Jeremy grabbed Ronnie by the hand and dragged him onto the dance floor, to the amusement of the girls. As much as they accepted the lifestyle their friends led, it still felt strange to watch two men waltzing together.

Stacey's eyes moved from Jeremy and Ronnie and were drawn to the couple dancing next to them. For the second time that evening, her jaw dropped in astonishment. When she turned to Belle, she noticed the same reaction on her friend's face.

"Do you see what I see?" Belle asked.

"I'm afraid so."

"I can't believe it."

"Neither can I," Stacey gasped.

There, just a few feet in front of her, wrapped in the arms of another man while swaying slowly to the music, was the man she loved. The sight was so absurd to her that she went from shock to tears and laughter in the span of minutes.

"Why are you laughing?" Belle asked.

"Because I was racking my brain over the past two days wondering if there was another woman in Dane's life. It turns out that I won't have to worry about that anymore."

"You're taking this rather well."

"Yeah, I guess I am," Stacey replied with a smile.

On the one hand, her heart was breaking and she was mortified to see Dane in the arms of his male partner. On the other hand, his sexual orientation made the rejection less insulting. It wasn't that he had no interest in her—he had no interest in her entire gender. She could now stop taking his indifference so personally and work on maintaining their working relationship and, in time, their friendship.

By noon the next day, Stacey had completed the final story for her manuscript. It was about two co-workers who tried to resist the attraction they had for one another, but in the end they fell in love, and once again the heroine ended up with Mr. Right. She prayed that one day her life would replicate one of her stories and she would have her own happily ever after.

Four Days in July

ROBERT HUNT

Author's Note: Many years after the sinking of the SS Venture, *this story's merchant marine sailor, Edward Hunt, remembered his friends and the sinking as though it were yesterday. Edward had contacted many of the survivors throughout the years. He never forgot the fifty-nine men lost nor the thirty-three who lived. He told me of his ordeal only once, over Christmas of 1988, two years before his death. I guess now, in his passing, his shipwrecked days at sea have finally been put to rest. I, for one, hope that they have.*

LISA IVANY and ROBERT HUNT

I will never forget this beautiful evening as I stare out through the Narrows in the port of St. John's, Newfoundland, as we ready our ship, the SS *Venture*, for sail on the open sea. Everything is so quiet and peaceful as I study the serenity around me. The sun dips behind the clouds as they settle on the hills that overlook the harbour, and continues its trek over the horizon before dropping into a misty haze of dew and darkness. A hint of rain is in the air as we breathe it in, and dozens of seagulls fly perilously close to us. The water in the harbour has a calm to it that I have never seen before. I feel a chill as I stand on deck and think how quiet the night is. I keep trying to ignore the ominous feeling that must go through all sailors' minds as they prepare to leave home and go to war, a feeling that, once they leave their homeland and their loved ones, they may never return to see them again. It is quiet here, but there is a war raging overseas.

It is July 2, 1942, and I find myself in awe as I look about the port of St. John's and see ships from many nations making preparations for war. Flags of every colour and from all corners of the world are fluttering in the breeze as men rush back and forth aboard their ships, readying to make sail for the open sea. I wonder why I am here aboard this ship today and look skyward for a sign. The realization strikes me that we are about to fight an enemy I do not even know, one I have never met. I think, while I lean over the ship's railing, *Why has God chosen, me, a young man from Harbour*

Breton, to fight overseas and to face what I do not even understand? I leave my future in His Hands.

Upon departure, my thoughts drift to my wife, Mary Carmel, and to how much I will miss her.

I glance back at St. John's as the *Venture* eases out through the Narrows, and it is then that it dawns on me that I might be sailing off to my death. My thoughts are with Mary, and Newfoundland, and whether I will ever return to see them again. I imagine these things, family and home, have entered the minds of all young men and women who have departed to an unknown fate. What lies ahead is not in our hands but controlled by others. As the land disappears from my sight, I wonder if I have made the right decision, but I know now that it is too late to change what I have set in motion by enlisting in the navy. I resign myself to the fact that it was I who had volunteered to fight in this war. I maintain that I have done this for the right reasons and that I am fighting for a just cause.

We have been on the high seas for three days; we are told that our final destination is somewhere in the English Channel near Dover, England. The day starts poorly, with several of the men suffering from food poisoning. Luckily, I have been spared since as I was not hungry last night and had only some tea and biscuits before bedtime. Things are tense these past few days, as we have made several radar sightings of German U-boats in our immediate area. We pray that they are only passing by, that they have larger targets in mind than our supply ships.

Some of the men have taken sick, so I have drawn double duty on the port side of the ship. With binoculars in hand, we have to be on the lookout for enemy patrols and watch for torpedo sightings. The days are not too bad. We can see the missiles if they are launched toward us in the water, but with dusk comes the unknown. This could happen at a moment's notice. We all fear for the safety of our crew and ship.

On our fourth day at sea, one of our crew members has died. He was an older man. The doctor thinks he had a heart condition and therefore should not have enlisted; somehow he had passed the physical. We will never know for sure, as he will be buried at sea, never to return home to his family in Newfoundland. As we slip him into the cold water, I think that, at least now, for him the war is over.

We have seen many signs of battle in the distant sky. We are given a nightly light show, and feel that it is only a matter of time before we become involved in the fighting ourselves. The crew has gotten more comfortable aboard the ship, but we feel tense as we move closer to our destination. We will soon reach the shores of Dover—and the war zone. I wonder what England will look like as fate draws us closer to the conflict.

This war brings a fear to the crew they have never known before, and we have terrible nightmares and suffer sleepless nights. My dreams of imminent danger do not leave me. I try to suppress my feelings, but I fear what tomorrow will bring. Newfoundland is left far behind, but the memories of home keep me going. I take out a picture of Mary Carmel, and it helps me forget what lies ahead.

This morning the sun's rays stretch out beautifully over the Atlantic Ocean. I walk up the gangway from below deck, when a sharp, shrilling crack makes me spin around. When I look behind me, I see water chasing my heels. I rush up the steps and turn once more, and that is when I see my friend, Danny, engulfed in water. His eyes plead with me to help him. He tries to scream, but no sound comes out. He tries to climb the stairs, but instead is dragged helpless into the water. I leap onto the deck, and immediately am propelled into the air by a thunderous blast. There is nothing but pain and darkness as a floating sensation fills me. I drift back down into the sea and the water swallows me. I see Mary Carmel's hand reaching for me; I wonder what she is doing here. I float toward her, but the cold, dark sea pushes me toward the surface of the water and sunlight. My head hurts terribly—I feel as if someone is hitting me in the face.

All is spinning as a piece of wood slides beneath me. I grab it in a dazed state. I try to focus on the voice that seems to be calling my name. "Hold on, Ned, hold on." I am drawn aboard a piece of wreckage, and I am disappointed to find out that it is not Mary Carmel, but Ellis, the ship's cook, who is clutching my shirt. *Why is he holding me so tightly?* As he pushes me farther onto the wreckage toward another shipmate, another noise breaks the silence and again we are pushed high into the air. I feel as if I am weightless. My friend and I slam back into the sea with a hard smack. Not fully aware of my surroundings, I resurface and look for my two companions. They are not there, having been swept off the wreckage and probably to their deaths. I periodically hear voices and know that something is seriously wrong. I try to focus as I look around me. There is no movement and time seems to stand still. I lay my head down and close my eyes.

    I drift in and out of sleep for what seems an eternity, and finally my eyes open to a placid sun staring down on me. I think my mind is playing tricks on me as I try to make sense of what is happening. *Am I going mad? Have my senses left me?* I roll to one side and my eyes adjust to my surroundings. Then comes the sound of talking around me and my head hurts terribly. I realize that I am with other men on a piece of debris from our sunken vessel. I see that many of my shipmates are clinging to similar pieces of flotsam. It is then that I finally realize what has happened. We have been torpedoed!

    I close my eyes again, but the screaming inside my head does not want to stop. I think of my friends who were swept

AT HEART

into the sea and I start to cry. Tears flow from my eyes and I slowly make the sign of the cross. I cry for Danny, Harold, and Johnny. My wish is go to sleep and not ever wake. My thoughts are jumbled. I move about with great difficulty and look for other survivors. Though I am dizzy, I manage to pull Pat, Gerald, and David onto the wreckage with me. I continue to search and see many of our men floating in the water, dead. I cannot stop crying. I have never felt so alone. I lay down, close my eyes, and drift off once again.

Later, I feel someone touching me. *Am I dead? I must be in Heaven and an angel is touching me, for have I not been a good man on this earth?* Someone is touching my head and talking to me. When my senses focus I am told by Byron, one of the survivors, that I have been asleep for most of the day and I was talking of Newfoundland and Mary Carmel. I recall small pieces of what happened after the explosion. Somehow I do remember, with extreme clarity, the loss of many of my friends. May God have mercy on them all! Survivors are now afloat on the ship's wreckage and in the two lifeboats the crew has managed to get into the water before the *Venture* sank. First Mate Lewis is still alive and tells me that only thirty-three of the ninety-two men aboard are alive and accounted for. He tells me that the submarine that torpedoed us surfaced and looked at us for a while before diving below the surface of the water and leaving us all to perish. Byron speaks fluent German. He says the captain of the U-boat stopped his gunners from shooting the survivors. I say a prayer for those who have perished. I know that they are all with God this day. We fear that the other ships' crews in our convoy believe us all dead, because we have not seen anyone since the explosion. Surely all were not sunk?

Days pass while we drift on the debris. We take turns getting into the two lifeboats to keep warm at night. Are we to be abandoned to the sea? My head is still pounding and I find it hard to concentrate as my friends chatter nearby. I fall in and out of sleep as the names of the missing are tabulated by the captain. I pray for each of the missing. I pray that the Lord will not forsake us, the thirty-three survivors floating out here in the Atlantic Ocean. I take out the picture of Mary Carmel and stare at it endlessly, wishing I were with her in Newfoundland.

On the fourth day adrift, we sight some ships off in the distance, but too far for them to see us. We eat some of the meagre rations salvaged from the *Venture*. My headaches are an everyday occurrence now. I long for home and my dreams are forever with my wife. I hope that news has not reached her of the ship's sinking, for I fear she would think I am lost. My worry is of never seeing her again and of the family I will never have if I perish here at sea. I pray again for God not to desert us in our time of need. With few supplies and hardly any water, we cannot last very long.

Finally, after days adrift and with evening approaching, we are spotted by cargo ships, with military escorts, heading toward Dover with supplies for the war effort. We shoot off a small flare we have saved from the *Venture*. It attracts their attention and they speed toward us. My guess is we will soon set foot on solid ground and this nightmare will end. Many things enter my mind as my friends and I are helped aboard our rescue ship. I hear my friends talking of home as I settle down, wrapped in several blankets, on the deck. I soon drift off to sleep, and the same nightmares scome to me again.

The two weeks that I spent at Dover in a military hospital have brought me relief from my injuries. My headaches are constant, but the doctors feel that the migraines should lessen after my head wounds and facial cuts start to heal. While I am recovering, I witness first-hand what the horror of war does to the men and women who serve in it. I see the agony and suffering of those who lie sick and wounded in the hospital. Limbs are lost. I shudder as I look at the victims in their beds. As I walk from ward to ward, I see many people who will never return home and those who will die in a strange country fighting for what they believe in. I thank God I am not one of them. War will leave scars on me that will never heal, and I will go home a different man than when I left Newfoundland such a short time ago. Mary Carmel has been notified that I am alive and well and waiting to be discharged. Time seems to stand still as I wait to go home. Weeks earlier I could not wait to see England, but now I cannot wait to leave it. I was told by a Red Cross nurse that I will know tomorrow the date of my discharge. Tonight, I fall asleep dreaming of Mary Carmel and home.

At sunrise, I am notified that we sail for Newfoundland at week's end. I can envision my wife waiting for me in St. John's harbour as I sail into port aboard a military destroyer. I walk to the window and stare out at the ocean. I think of all my friends who were lost at sea aboard the SS *Venture* and know that I will never see them again. I see their faces and hear their laughter in my sleep. Those men who were alive only a short time ago, those who spoke of their loved ones and of this terrible war . . . now they are all gone. I seem to cry a lot these days. I bless myself as I stand by the hospital window, knowing that I will never forget what has happened to the men with whom I have served. I will be with them, in spirit, always.

Moon Rider

LISA IVANY and ROBERT HUNT

Hank Penashue was deep in thought as he walked along the grassy field toward the tents that were staggered along the St. Lawrence River. He ran his olive-skinned fingers through his coal-black hair and looked skyward. Several dark clouds had moved westward, away from the group that had gathered along the riverbank. It seemed that the sky would clear; a good sign of things to come that day, he hoped.

He strolled toward a group of people who were conversing near the water. Hank knew that the meetings over the next few days had to be productive in order to convince his employer of the need for a rehab centre for his people. Many friends and relatives had been enslaved by addictions for as long as he could remember, and Hank wanted to help break the cycle.

LISA IVANY and ROBERT HUNT

The day was July 26, 1988, the day of the annual pilgrimage the Innu people made to the Basilica of Sainte-Anne-de-Beaupré. Hank had not attended the event for over eight years, nor been home during that time. He wondered what type of reception he would receive upon addressing the tribal elders the following day. Standing a short distance from the field of canvas tents that had been erected for the event, Hank wondered how the elders could be convinced to support the endeavour. The twenty-six-year-old man's dark brown eyes stared rigidly under creased thick brows. He questioned the decision to be here in Quebec City.

His last memory of home in Sheshatshiu was of being escorted in handcuffs to the back of an RCMP wagon for drunk and disorderly conduct and damaging property. The wagon had been packed with the six other perpetrators in their group, who were so wasted on drugs and alcohol they probably didn't realize the depth of the trouble they were in. Certainly, Hank's two best friends, Louis Osmond and Charlie Dyke, were in high spirits as they laughed about how they had thrown rocks and broken several windows of Chief McKenzie's house.

Drugs and drinking were a part of life for many of the youth in the Innu community. The teens had committed various offenses over the years and went virtually unpunished, but an example would soon be made of these young members of the Tundra band. The police had reached their breaking point with the rowdy teenagers. The destruction of property this time would finally give them legitimate reason to lay charges. As it turned out, the court sentenced the teenagers to undergo treatment at a detox centre in St. John's. They were not permitted outside the building for the duration of the treatment, and they had to participate in every group meeting or they would be given jail time.

When the program concluded, the tribal elders decided their fate and gave each of them the choice of returning to Sheshatshiu or accepting a grant from the government to attend Memorial University or a school of their choice. Hank and a few others opted for the latter, but some friends had gone back home. Hank had not been in contact with them since.

"Moon Rider!" a voice yelled, interrupting his thoughts.

Hank turned at the sound of his Innu nickname. There was his old friend, Charlie Dyke, barrelling across the open field toward him. Charlie embraced his long-lost friend in an enthusiastic hug that nearly took Hank's breath away.

"Moon Rider! Is that really you?"

"Yes, Fox Chaser, it's me," Hank replied, using Charlie's Innu name. "It's been a long time."

"Too long, my friend. I heard you graduated two years ago and you're a social worker now. I'm happy for you, Hank, but I've often wondered why you never returned home, even during the holidays."

Hank turned his gaze to the ground. "The answer to that is twofold. First, I was too ashamed to face the community, especially Chief Mackenzie, after what we had done to his home. Secondly, I feared that once I went home I would slip into the same routine with the old gang and not want to go back to school. I didn't want to disappoint my parents any further, so I stayed in St. John's and worked as an addictions counsellor after graduation."

"Well, I'm glad you're here for the celebration," Charlie said.

"How about you? What have you been up to since I've been gone, Fox Chaser?"

"Oh, not much, but I did stop drinking and getting into trouble. I'm a logger now, and I married a wonderful lady who changed my life." Charlie laughed. "Come over this evening to our tent and meet my family. Shanet has some roasted caribou cooking and the bannock should be ready by now. She has a special way of frying the bread that puts the older women to shame."

Hank grinned. "Sounds too good to resist."

As he walked from one tent to another, Hank found that any earlier misgivings were unwarranted as he was greeted with warm smiles and embraces from the people of Sheshatshiu. Catching up on old times with the people from home proved to be very relaxing. He participated in religious rituals and social activities, abstaining from any form of alcohol as he had done for the past eight years. However, Hank soon realized that many present enjoyed more than just a social drink. They seemed to be in a continuous state of inebriation, even during the morning and midday hours. *Things have not changed much*, he thought.

At the meetings later that evening, a few of the men argued about conditions in their areas. Bart Abraham, a counsellor from Hopedale, was exciting some of the crowd. It was obvious the man had been drinking. Hank feared trouble would brew when the meetings started to get more serious over the next few days. He felt that Bart would cause problems if his community did not receive a grant for its own rehabilitation centre. Bart's intoxication was somewhat ironic, pushing as he was for a government-funded alcohol and drug rehab centre for his hometown. Hank hadn't revealed that one of his own reasons for returning was to assess the need for the opening of that same service in Sheshatshiu. Only two out of four areas of Labrador would receive these grants. Essentially, Hank and Bart were rivals.

When he wearied of the drunken revelry, Hank slipped away into the midday sun and found a quiet place to work by the riverbank. He sat cross-legged upon a raised mound of grass-covered earth shaded by a large granite boulder. While dictating a report, he sensed a presence beside him.

"Who are you talking to?" a woman's voice asked.

Startled, Hank turned to see a figure blocking out part of the sun. He shaded his eyes.

"I'm just recording some notes for work," he replied.

Her long black hair glistened in the sun's rays, and the

headdress with white and turquoise feathers she wore accentuated her olive skin and brown eyes. A white, feather-trimmed, rawhide dress fell to just below her ankles, above a pair of beaded suede sandals. She was a vision of beauty, Hank thought.

"Hi, my name is Sunflower."

"I'm Hank Penashue, but my friends call me Moon Rider."

"I haven't seen you here before, Moon Rider. Is this your first time attending the celebration?" Sunflower asked, seating herself on the grass beside him.

"No. I just haven't been here for several years while I was away at university, and then work commitments didn't allow me time off to come."

"It seems you still have work commitments even though you are here," Sunflower commented while pointing at his hand-held transcriber.

Hank laughed. "Guilty as charged."

"May I ask what your association is with the people here?"

"I'm trying to develop a youth-addictions program for my people. I was told by the council elders that if I attended the meetings here they would listen to what I had to say with an open mind."

"That goal is to be commended, Hank, and I wish you luck. You will surely need it."

"I can only try, and hope that I'm successful," Hank answered.

Over the course of the afternoon, they spoke about the

upcoming sessions and how they could benefit the teens in Sheshatshiu. Although Sunflower agreed with Hank's views, she wondered if the council would be as easy to persuade.

"Well, I have to get back to my uncle's tent for the ceremonial band greeting," Sunflower said. "It was nice meeting you. Maybe we will see each other during the proceedings."

"The pleasure was all mine," Hank replied.

The young woman danced across the field, her long hair bouncing upon her back. As she neared the compound of tents, she turned and waved to Hank.

Cupping his hands around his mouth, Hank yelled, "I'll be here again at sunset if you'd like to come back and talk."

He wasn't sure if Sunflower had heard him, but hoped that she had, for he yearned to discover more about this beautiful woman. Hank silently cursed himself. He had been so wrapped up in discussing his work that he hadn't even discovered her real name or what band she was from. He knew virtually nothing about her, and wanted to know everything. Hank was still daydreaming about this feathered princess when he felt a jab in his side.

"Hey, Moon Rider, what were you talking to Sunflower about?" Charlie asked.

"Not much, just about the upcoming meetings, Charlie. Do you know her?" Hank asked hopefully.

"Yes. She's Caroline McKenzie, Chief McKenzie's niece. She was originally from Davis Inlet, but went to live with her uncle in Sheshatshiu a couple of years ago."

Hank's dreams of spending time with Sunflower were dashed. There was no way a Tundra boy would be permitted to associate with a McKenzie girl, especially when he had helped destroy her uncle's home eight years ago.

That evening, Sunflower *did* return to the place where they had met that morning. Hank sensed her presence behind him as the sun slowly dropped below the far horizon. They struck up a conversation that turned into a three-hour talk about the meetings and the necessity for rehabilitation centres back home.

"Why did you decide to return to your people now?" Sunflower asked Hank. "And why did you stay away so long after graduating?"

"I don't know. I guess that for years while I was away at school I didn't know what I wanted to do." He couldn't very well tell her that he was one of the people who had damaged her uncle's house . . . the very home in which she now lived. "When I heard about the possibility of getting a grant for a youth addictions program for Sheshatshiu, I knew I wanted to be involved. I have missed my people, and the longer I was away the more I missed them. After a while I knew the time was right to come home and put my education to good use by helping my people."

"I admire that . . . a man on a mission." Sunflower smiled, revealing perfect, pearl-white teeth.

Talking, they realized they had very similar goals and plans for the future. Before departing, Hank asked

AT HEART

Sunflower if she wished to accompany him to the dance on Saturday night. She said, teasingly, that she would let him know on the last day of the meetings.

That night, Hank's dreams were of Sunflower. He dreamed they were walking hand in hand across an open plain, when suddenly Sunflower's hand slipped from his and she ran a short distance ahead. He called her name, but no sound came out. She continued walking farther and farther ahead, and Hank was unable to catch her. He broke into a run, but still couldn't catch her. Finally, when he did manage to close the distance between them, Sunflower stopped and pointed to a distant ridge that bore the angry likeness of Bart Abraham. When she turned toward Hank, there was blood dripping from her cheek. Then she disappeared completely, and he stood alone.

For the rest of the night, sleep eluded Hank and the images from the dream tormented him. Closing his eyes, he saw either Bart's fearsome image or a wounded Sunflower.

The next day's meeting started at nine o'clock and dragged slowly on to one o'clock before the council called a break for lunch. All through the meetings, Bart Abraham, still loud and growing more agitated with each glass of spirits, kept looking at Hank in a way that made him wary.

The longer the meetings ran, the more it seemed that Bart started to downplay all the things that other members seemed to agree on. After many hours of discussion, Hank and the leaders had become totally frustrated with the way Bart was stirring up the crowd. They knew that something was about to happen. Whatever it was, Hank was sure to end up in the middle of it. By four o'clock, the session had stalled and Chief MacKenzie adjourned for the day.

Hank and Sunflower had arranged to meet at eight o'clock that evening, and going back to his quarters, Hank felt very happy at the way things were going between them. As the hours passed, his mind wandered away from the events of the day and all he could think of was seeing Sunflower again. He left his tent and went to meet her by the large boulder where they first met. He waited until nine o'clock, but she did not appear. Hank resigned himself to a long, lonely night.

As he neared the compound, someone grabbed his arm. It was a tribal elder. The man told Hank that several men of the Tundra clan, along with some from another group, the Musquaro Clan, were drinking and causing trouble at the meeting house. Also, Chief Mackenzie and several of the tribal leaders were there trying to keep order. Hank rushed to the council area to help.

He spotted Chief Mackenzie and Sunflower speaking with some of the women from the tribes. Approaching, Hank noticed that Bart Abraham was making a path toward the group as well. He stopped and watched as Bart spoke to Chief Mackenzie with heated words. After a few seconds, Hank watched as Sunflower said something to Bart. In an instant, the drunk man turned and raised his hand as if to strike, but instead pushed her aside. He looked at her with ferocious eyes.

"In our tribe the woman does not speak unless she is spoken to," Bart snarled. "This is men's business and you are not to interfere. Go back to the other women."

Hank had seen enough. In an instant, he jumped in, grabbed Bart by the arm, and turned him around so that both men faced each other. The anger in Bart's eyes was now fully on him. He was larger and stronger than Hank, but he could see that Hank would not back down from him.

"That's enough, Bart!" Hank snapped. "We are here to find a peaceful solution to our problems and not to cause more. I do not like the way you treat women, especially Sunflower. She is my friend and equal in status with anyone here, including you."

Bart turned his back to Hank, as if to ignore him, and began speaking to Chief Mackenzie. Suddenly, the larger man whipped around in a full 180-degree arc. Hank didn't see the blade sweep through the air until it was too late. It slashed across his face, and he backed away as blood dripped from the gash to the ground. Bart smiled and lunged again, but this time he was too slow. With lightning reflexes, Hank turned his body, and heard the blade slice through the air. As Bart swung to the left, Hank came up with a knee and caught the larger man in the side. There was a sound of cracking bone, and Bart went to his knees in pain. Hank stood over his adversary and waited for a counterattack. Bart clutched his side and lay gasping for breath, but still held the knife and waved it at Hank in a threatening manner.

Bart stood and sprang at Hank again, thrusting the blade forward with a vengeance. Hank was ready for it. He grabbed Bart's left arm, came up with his right, and caught Bart squarely on the jaw. His hand was a blur as he caught Bart under the chin with another quick blow to the face. The force of the punch knocked Bart to the ground again. This time, it was over. Bart lay defeated.

Looking at the crowd, Hank said, "This was not the way I planned to introduce myself here. These meetings are supposed to be done in peace and understanding amongst our people to unite as one. People like this should never be allowed to attend; they only come here to cause trouble and discontent. Bart and his followers should be banned from all future sessions so we can all negotiate and find a peaceful solution to our problems."

Chief Mackenzie looked at Hank with great admiration. Sunflower also caught his attention and smiled. After the crowd had thinned and Bart and his friends were ordered to leave, she walked over to Hank and attended to the cut on his face.

When they concluded the meetings that day, without Bart and his followers around, many of the policies that were presented were agreed upon. Hank figured this was

AT HEART

the time to speak to Chief Mackenzie concerning his feelings for Sunflower. He approached the elder and asked to have an audience. When they were alone, Hank addressed his concern.

"Chief Mackenzie, I have been here since the start of these proceedings and have grown very fond of your niece. I know it is not permitted by some tribal leaders for the Tundra and Mackenzie bands to mix." He paused a moment before continuing. "But with the greatest of respect, sir, I would like to ask your permission to see more of Sunflower in the future."

Chief Mackenzie smiled at Hank. "What you did today, and the way you handled yourself when trouble was present, shows me that you are a man of honour and peace. In fact, because of you, my leaders and I will be voting for the rehabilitation centre to be built in Sheshatshiu. Now, regarding my niece, you have my blessing to see her, but only if that is her wish as well."

From the deeply intimate stare Sunflower had been sending Hank from across the room, the chief knew that would not be a problem.

As Hank and Sunflower left the tent, hand in hand, Chief Mackenzie called out, "Moon Rider, there is one condition to my agreement."

"What is that?" he asked, confused.

"You must promise me there will be no rock-throwing in your future."

"You have my utmost promise on that, sir," Hank said stiffly. Then Chief Mackenzie burst into laughter.

On July 26, 1989, Moon Rider and Sunflower stood on the very mound of grass where they had met one year before. Since that day, Sheshatshiu had been awarded one of the grants for the community rehabilitation centre, and Hank had returned to take the position of Youth Addictions Counsellor. Getting the service for his area was not an easy task, and he learned that the job would be an ongoing battle to educate teenagers to the dangers of drug and alcohol addiction. He still wore the battle scar on his face from Bart Abraham's blade, but Hank felt it was worth it, as the end sometimes did justify the means.

This year, the field was covered with tents for the annual pilgrimage, but the majority of people had also gathered in one area to witness the joining of the McKenzie and Tundra bands as one. The sun spread its golden rays over the gathering, and there was a comfortable whisper of wind as Moon Rider and Sunflower exchanged vows and became man and wife. It was indeed a day for celebration.

Intern With A Secret

LISA IVANY

"Zak, since you're not on call tonight, let's go to Studio 12 and catch a movie," Lena suggested.

"Miss Vincent, that would be scandalous!" Zak replied.

"Why?"

"Someone from the hospital might see us together, and then the rumours would fly."

"So what if someone sees us together," she retaliated.

"I just don't want to give the gossips anything to talk about. My personal life is private and I'd like to keep it that way."

"Zak O'Connor, I don't know if I'll ever figure you out, and maybe I'm tired of trying," she fumed.

Lena sprang from the table next to the front door of the

cafeteria, nearly toppling her cup and saucer. She sped to the conveyer belt to dispose of her dishes from the morning's coffee break and darted through the side door to avoid passing Zak's long, lanky frame on the way out.

Zak watched Lena walk away and knew he had hurt her once again, but was helpless to do anything about it. He wanted to explain the reasons for not publicizing their relationship, but knew doing so would place her in great peril. That was a risk he was not willing to take.

He had met Lena six months ago, when he moved to St. John's to start a third-year residency training at the Health Sciences Complex. Zak was twenty-nine and she was older, thirty-six, but the age difference didn't bother either of them.

His first rotation had been in orthopaedics, and he was scheduled to assist Dr. Warren Martin with two major back surgeries on his first day. He remembered how nervous he was slipping into a scrub suit, and the difficulty he had tying the strings with his trembling hands. Zak was of a nervous disposition on a normal day—people called him skittish—but that day was the most stressful yet. He wanted to earn Dr. Martin's respect, but with two complicated back surgeries on the roster, he feared messing something up.

Zak pulled a cotton cap over his pale, shaved head and donned sterile gloves. His grey-blue eyes darted quickly about the scrub room and he chewed the insides of his lips in his customary nervous habit. He jumped when an unknown pair of hands reached up from behind and wrapped a mask around his face.

When he turned to thank his aide, he looked into the deepest set of sapphire-blue eyes he had ever seen. Her long, auburn ringlets were tucked beneath her cap, and thick black lashes and delicate rosy lips gave her the appearance of a porcelain doll, one that he instantly wanted to hold.

"Thanks for your help," Zak said. "I can't believe I forgot to put on the mask."

"This is your first day, isn't it?"

"Yeah, I guess it must be easy to tell," he laughed. "I'm Zak O'Connor."

"Oh yes, you're the new resident working with Dr. Martin this morning," she replied. "I'm Lena Vincent, porter for the operating room."

That was six months ago, Zak reminisced as he stared at the doorway Lena had just gone through. She was a magnet, drawing him closer and closer . . . an entity that couldn't be resisted, no matter how hard he tried. Even on days working in the outpatient clinic, Zak would find excuses to visit the O.R., just to be near her. Lena must have thought him scatterbrained, he thought, for the numerous times he told her he had left his stethoscope behind.

He knew Lena deserved better than the way he was treating her, but couldn't tell her his reasons for keeping their relationship a secret. He wanted to tell her, but couldn't risk losing her for good. She was having a hard enough time trying to understand why he wouldn't stay overnight at her place. They were intimate, to a point, but Zak would pull back before things got too involved. He told her it was because he didn't want to rush things, and although Lena said she respected his decision, he sensed she was unhappy.

Just after four o'clock, Zak went to the switchboard to turn in his pager and noticed the desk calendar. It was February 14, Valentine's Day, and he wondered if flowers would help get him back into Lena's good graces this evening, and if he was still expected to go to her place for dinner. She had invited him yesterday, but that was before their first official spat in the cafeteria this morning.

The yellow Ford Mustang pulled out into the rush-hour traffic of Prince Philip Drive, and Zak impatiently cursed his slow progress. It was times like these he wished to be back home in Morpeth, Ontario. With a population of 300, there was never a problem with traffic. He turned on the CD player and his favourite song, "100 Years To Live." As he sang along, he found his body relaxing, and by the time he arrived at the florist's he was in good spirits.

Zak knocked on the door of Lena's bungalow on Pearson Street at six o'clock, bracing himself for a cool reception. However, when she saw the twelve long-stemmed red roses and heart-shaped box of truffles he held, her smile was genuine.

"Oh, Zak, they're beautiful!" she exclaimed as she inhaled the scent of the perfumed petals.

"Does this mean I'm still invited to dinner?"

"You probably shouldn't be," she pouted. "However, I can't resist flowers and chocolate."

"Happy Valentine's Day, Lena."

She answered by wrapping her arms around Zak's neck and pulling his lips to hers for a long, intimate kiss. The earlier disagreement was completely forgotten.

Later that night, they lay together on the sofa, arms and legs tightly intertwined, watching a double feature. When the second movie ended, Zak slowly climbed over his couchmate and rose to his feet. He pulled her up into his embrace and probed her mouth delicately with his tongue. Without breaking the kiss, he gradually backed down the hallway, pulling her with him, before he slipped into his boots.

"It's pretty late," Lena said. "Why don't you stay the night?"

Zak hesitated.

"Well, no one knows you're here."

"No, but my roommate will wonder where I've been when I don't show up until morning," he replied.

"Who cares?" Lena huffed. "Zak, I'm tired of feeling like I'm your dirty little secret. You won't go out in public with me and you don't want anyone to know you're here. I don't understand why you're ashamed of me."

"It's not that," he murmured. "I just think we should be discreet for a while, to see where things are going with us before we let the world know, okay?"

"I have a better idea," she replied sharply. "When you

decide to grow up and become a real man, give me a call. Until then, you don't have to worry about hiding our relationship, because there won't be one to hide!"

Lena yanked the door wide, shoved Zak through, and slammed the bolt shut. The cold air hit him in the face with a blast, but it didn't sting like her words. He felt as if the wind had just been kicked out of him as the full impact of what she had said sank in. He bowed his head and stared at his feet, contemplating whether he should leave or stay.

"Hurry up and leave, Dr. O'Connor!" Lena yelled from behind the door. "If anyone sees you here, that would be scandalous!"

Her sarcasm was not lost on Zak, and he knew she was speaking from hurt—hurt that he had inflicted. From her tone, he knew there was no chance she would unlatch the door and let him back inside tonight. He pressed the remote starter and the Mustang roared to life on the quiet street. Berating himself for not starting the car earlier, he grabbed the ice scraper and spent the next fifteen minutes beating chunks of freezing rain off the windshield.

Zak had noticed a black SUV parked down the road when he came out of Lena's. The lights were off, but the engine was running. It made him a little uneasy at first, but he reasoned the driver could be heating the car or waiting to pick someone up. However, by the time Zak was ready to drive off, he noticed that no one had gotten into or out of the car at any time . . . and that made him nervous.

AT HEART

He was nearly to the end of the street when a bright light hit his rear-view mirror. Zak was momentarily blinded by the truck's high beams. He turned down his mirror to dull the glare and pressed on the brake as he neared a stop sign. He pumped the brake several times, but the car was not slowing down. *Oh my God, the brakes are gone!* his mind screamed. Holding his breath, he veered the car left onto Torbay Road. Luckily, at this time of night, the traffic was very light and he made the turn safely.

Zak maintained a speed of fifty, but was unable to slow down any further. The SUV continued to follow him, its headlights filling the interior of the car. Smash! Zak's head jerked backward from the impact of the vehicle behind. The jolt forced the Mustang to accelerate and spin out of control as it was propelled onto Elizabeth Avenue. He knew now that the brakes had not malfunctioned—they had been tampered with.

Zak had been keeping a low profile for six months, to the point of changing his name and shaving his head in an effort to disguise his identity, but somehow he had been discovered. It would take a miracle to get out of this alive. The street was quiet now, but during the day the area reverberated with jackhammers, cranes, and other ongoing construction. He saw the detour signs up ahead where a section of road had been dug up. The flashing yellow lights displayed arrows in the direction of the detour, where a deep pit surrounded by slabs of broken asphalt had been roped off.

When Zak tried to manoeuvre the car toward the detour, the SUV sped up to his side of the car and slammed against it, sending Zak directly into the pit. The car nosedived into the hollow excavation, accompanied by the sounds of crashing metal and splintering glass on impact. Zak painstakingly turned his head to the left and peered up through the crevice he had just plummeted into. A stocky, white-haired man in a black trench coat stood next to the yellow flashing markers, pointing a pistol at Zak's head. However, the sound of approaching voices changed the assailant's plans, forcing him into concealment. The last thing Zak noticed before losing consciousness was the patch over the man's right eye.

"Zak, it's time to wake up." A voice spoke to him as though from deep within a dream. "Zak, can you hear me?"

He tried to focus on the voice and, after several failed attempts, opened his eyes.

"That's better. We thought you were going to sleep all day," Dr. Martin laughed. "How are you feeling?"

"A little light-headed actually. Where am I?"

"You're in emergency. All your vitals are good and you have no fractures. It's a miracle you came out of the accident alive."

"Yeah, I guess I didn't see the detour until it was too late," he lied. Zak couldn't explain what had actually transpired, not without putting others in jeopardy.

When the test results came back negative, Zak was discharged and given a slip to stay off work for a couple of days to recuperate. He couldn't go home because "Patch" would probably be staking out his house, waiting to finish the job. He also knew that Lena's place was no longer safe. Now she was in danger, too, and he must convince her to leave her apartment, at least for the time being.

Zak went to the operating room and found her alone in the supply closet.

"I just heard about your accident and I was on my way to see you," she said, worry evident in her eyes. "Are you okay?"

"Yes, I'm fine, especially now that you're talking to me."

"I was just concerned about a fellow co-worker's health, that's all. Now that I know you're okay, there's no need to talk further," she quipped. "Now, let's get out of here before someone sees us. That would be scandalous!"

"I don't care anymore," he replied as he pulled her into a tight embrace. He didn't even pull away when one of the nurses popped in to retrieve a kidney dish.

Although he had said he felt fine, Zak had some fairly extensive bruises and lacerations to his lower extremities and needed to rest. He lay in a curtained-off area of the recovery room on a gurney while Lena went to request the rest of the day off to take care of him. She was more than a little perplexed when he said they would have to check into a hotel rather than return home. When she refused to leave the hospital without more information, Zak told her he was being pursued by someone trying to kill him and she was in danger too. He was finally ready to tell her why he had been behaving so strangely, and promised to explain everything later.

"My leave is approved, so let's get going," Lena announced on her return.

"Thanks for doing this for me, honey."

It was the first time Zak had called her by anything other than her given name, and the endearment set her insides to fluttering. She thought maybe there was a chance for them after all, but she would make that judgment after he revealed his secret.

"We'd better hurry," Lena said. "There was someone at the nursing station asking for you and he looked suspicious."

Zak gingerly lifted one injured leg and then the other over the side of the mattress, ready to rise. He froze. Through the curtain's narrow opening, he saw the man with the eye patch walk by the recovery room door. *Any second he's going to find me and finish the job*, Zak thought.

Moments later, Lena wheeled the gurney down the corridor and staff members stepped aside to give ample room out of respect. They knew she was on her way to the morgue with the linen-covered body she was pushing. She looked a little anxious, but that was understandable; escorting dead bodies was not a task for the squeamish.

Lena rode the elevator to the basement. She was apprehensive about entering the morgue's cold, windowless room, especially when it would be dark and vacant this morning.

AT HEART

Since there were no autopsies scheduled, the pathologists would be in their offices upstairs doing paperwork.

A heavy silence surrounded Lena when the door to the morgue clicked shut behind her. She felt along the wall for a light switch, but her fingers only encountered cold cement blocks. Without the aid of windows, the room was pitched into absolute darkness, and she felt her heart was about to burst out of her chest with its intense pounding. She then remembered the light switch for the morgue was situated just outside the door in the hallway.

Lena turned around and crept to the door, slowly pulling it open and peering outside to ensure the coast was clear. With no one in sight, she reached out her hand and flicked on the switch before slinking back inside.

She caught movement from the corner of her eye and spun in that direction. Before her, on the nearest gurney, the body under the sheet had risen to a sitting position. Still completely clad in the white linen sheet, it gave the appearance of a ghost. She screamed.

"Quiet!" Zak called as he pulled down the sheet to reveal his face.

"Sorry," she apologized. "You frightened me."

Even now, with the rows of fluorescent tubing illuminating the room to reveal bare, stainless steel workstations, Lena felt her body shiver in protest. This sense of fear was heightened when the room was once again plunged into darkness. She hadn't seen Zak silently slip out and flick off the switch.

On his return to Lena's side, he said, "We don't want to attract unwanted attention with the lights on."

Zak realized there was only one exit from the morgue, so they would have to flee immediately or risk being cornered. With Lena's support, he hobbled to the door as fast as he could, but the handle turned before they reached it. The door opened slowly, and the shadow of a man filled the entryway. It advanced on Zak, who was now alone and leaning against a shelf to support his injuries.

"Are you Zak O'Connor?" the man asked, but he didn't get to hear the reply before collapsing to the floor. Lena had crept up from behind and, with all the strength she could muster, slammed a heavy metal tray against the back of his neck. She held the tray above her head, prepared to mete out further punishment if needed, but the man lay face down and motionless. Zak leaned down and rolled the man over to see his face.

From the thin sliver of light from the nearly closed door, he could see the man was clean-cut, with short dark hair.

"This isn't the guy who was after me," Zak stated.

"What do you mean?" Lena shrieked. "This is the same man who was asking for you at the nursing station upstairs."

"It's not him."

"Then who is he?"

"Someone's coming," Zak said.

The door swung open and the light from the hallway was

slowly swallowed up by a large shadow looming in the door frame. Zak and Lena's fears were realized when they looked into the face of the man with the patch. The man's girth and Zak's injured legs prohibited any chance of flight.

A single cold eye pierced the couple with its icy stare. The man's mouth curved into a malicious grin as he removed an object from his pocket. The appearance of the pistol produced a frightened squeal from Lena and a quick intake of breath from Zak. Patch methodically twisted the silencer around the end of the weapon's barrel, then raised the gun in their direction.

"Get back into the room," he ordered.

"Let her go and I'll do whatever you want," Zak pleaded.

"Sorry, this is not a negotiation," Patch said. "Now, do as I say."

As Zak and Lena reluctantly backed into the room, Patch flicked on the light switch and followed them in. His calculated expression revealed a man who enjoyed his occupation as a professional killer.

He noticed the man on the floor and stepped over him while forcing his victims farther into the room.

"I guess I should thank you for finally getting rid of this cop for me," Patch said, pointing the barrel of his weapon toward the unconscious man. "He's been a thorn in my side since I left Ontario—always right behind me."

Zak pushed Lena behind him and tried again to reason with the man.

"Please don't hurt her. She has nothing to do with this," he begged. "She doesn't even know what any of this is about, so please let her go."

"I can't do that," he replied. "She's a witness."

"A witness to what?" Zak asked.

"Why, your murder, of course," the man sneered. "You see, I plan to kill you first."

Zak pushed Lena behind him, as though this would protect her from the impending bullet, or at least buy her some time. The couple watched in terror as Patch aimed the gun at Zak's chest and started to squeeze the trigger.

"Freeze! This is the police!" a voice shouted from behind the gunman. "Drop your weapon."

Patch whirled around with his gun still raised and a shot rang out. He fell in a leaden heap to the floor.

"Are you two okay?" the officer asked.

"We are now," Zak replied as he tightened his hold on Lena.

"I'm really sorry for hitting you," Lena apologized. "I thought you were the one who was trying to kill Zak."

The officer laughed. "No harm done, except for a mild headache."

After taking their statements, the officer allowed them to go home. They went back to Lena's place, now deeming it to be safe. She helped Zak into bed, where he finally revealed the secret he had been keeping and why he didn't want their relationship to be discovered. He explained that anyone associated with him could potentially become a target as a way of getting to him.

It had all started three years ago, during his training as a clinical clerk at the General Hospital in Windsor, Ontario. Zak had finished his shift at midnight and had taken a shortcut home through an alley. He stopped when he heard voices arguing about a drug deal that had gone sour, and watched in horror as one man was silenced with a bullet from the other.

The killer was not aware of Zak's presence and didn't even know there was a witness until the trial. Although most of the evidence was circumstantial, Zak's account swayed the jury to submit a verdict of guilty, sending Freddy Gambodi to prison for life. However, the drug lord's attorney found a loophole in the case and won an appeal. The new trial was set to start in another week, and Zak would have to testify once again.

During his incarceration, Gambodi had sent several hired guns to eliminate Zak, because without his testimony, the criminal would undoubtedly be acquitted. Luckily, the case was high-profile, so the Drug Enforcement Division of the RCMP always had an officer nearby, keeping an eye on their star witness.

"That's unbelievable!" Lena stated when Zak had finished his narrative. "Are you still in danger?"

"Not anymore. The agent who rescued us today said they now have me under constant protection until the trial is over," he replied. "That means I will soon get back to having a normal life."

"Is there any room in your normal life for me?"

"A whole heartful of room," Zak said as he pulled her down beside him on the pillow.

Two months later, Zak and Lena sat across from each other in the dining room of the Delta Hotel. The trial had concluded two days earlier with another guilty verdict, and Zak had flown back from Ontario the same evening.

Several of their colleagues from the Health Sciences Complex were seated at a long table across the aisle. Apparently, it was Administrative Assistant's Day, and several physicians were treating their secretaries to dinner.

"I think we have an audience," Lena whispered.

"Well, I think we should give them a show," Zak replied.

"What do you mean?"

Without answering, he leaned across the table and captured Lena's lips with his own. The sound of clapping erupted from the next table as their colleagues cheered them on.

"That's scandalous!" Lena laughed.

"Yeah. Isn't it great?" Zak grinned as he moved in for another kiss.

Crossing the Tube

ROBERT HUNT

Amy sat alone in Captain Murphy's office, staring at the walls and the many awards and citations that adorned them. She was restless and could not find a comfortable position in the hard wooden chair. She tried to put what had occurred this past week into perspective. The reality of her current situation still had not sunk in, but she worried about the reason she had been summoned to the Captain's office. Deep in thought, Amy did not hear him enter the room. He sat down at his desk opposite her and took a brief moment to straighten his desk before speaking. The silence was deafening.

"I'll have to ask for your gun and badge, Officer Young," Captain Murphy said.

His words vibrated through the office. Amy couldn't believe what she was hearing! She took the gun and holster from her arm cradle and laid them on his desk, then unbuckled her badge from its protective Velcro pouch and put it next to the weapon. Amy never thought it would be like this. She felt like she was in someone else's dream and that she would wake up at any moment. The captain's stoic expression didn't change as he took Amy's gun and badge from the desk.

"I'm sorry, Amy, but until an internal investigation is concluded in this matter, I have no other choice but to assign you to a desk job here in the office."

"Captain, Sergeant Miller is making a mistake. You will see that when an inquiry takes place and I'm exonerated. You will also see that I did not cross the tube when we were in that house."

"Amy, you know I can't comment on or second-guess another police officer until I have more facts to help me make a decision on what's happened. Until all facts have been looked at and a conclusion reached, you will work here at the station."

Amy nodded. She knew he was right, but still felt sick to her stomach as she got up and headed out of his office. Things were happening too fast. She would have to slow down the process in order to protect her future with the police force.

Amy had been a police officer with the RCMP detachment in Clarenville for seven years now, and this was the first time she had ever faced any real adversity. Sure, there was the occasional sexist joke from other officers, but she always took it in stride . . . and gave as good as she got. For the most part, Amy was treated with respect by her fellow officers and knew that they would not look at her differently because she was a woman. There was only Sergeant Miller, who had always considered her an outsider but had never really said anything in the years that they had worked together. Maybe there was more going on behind her back than she knew. She and her fellow officers did patrols from Clarenville to Bonavista, and surrounding areas, and there hadn't been any trouble with them until this week. This week had been her personal nightmare.

She and her partner, Officer Derek Reynolds, had been responding to a domestic dispute in Lethbridge, when the incident went from bad to worse. Derek had drawn his weapon when the drunken owner of the home had become violent. Amy had lunged at the attacker to subdue him. Sergeant Miller, who had also responded to the dispute as backup, entered the house just as the melee began. Apparently, he had also drawn his weapon in an effort to make the owner step down from his attack. In the few moments that followed, the owner of the home was handcuffed and the confrontation ended peacefully.

Outside, Sergeant Miller told Amy that he would speak to Captain Murphy about laying charges against her, as she had "crossed the tube," a tactical expression meaning she had stepped in front of the barrel of a fellow officer's loaded weapon. She had not only endangered herself, Miller said, but had put him in a compromising position of possibly shooting or injuring a fellow officer in the line of duty. Amy was shocked and knew in her heart and soul that Miller was only going to lay charges because of reasons yet to be revealed. She hoped the inquiry and her partner's testimony would set things straight.

Amy had heard rumours about Miller's prejudices but had not thought anything of them until now. Jealousy was present in all workplaces, but it seemed to her now that the Sergeant was the only one on the Clarenville Police Force with an attitude toward women. Until recently, he had kept it to himself. Amy recalled how he always called her Officer Young, never Amy.

Amy had graduated second in her class at the police academy in Regina, Saskatchewan. After graduation, she spent two years at the Grand Falls–Windsor detachment, before being assigned to the Clarenville office. Numerous drug- and sex-related arrests in her first year had earned her due respect from her fellow officers, men and women alike, but Sergeant Miller had always seemed somewhat cold toward her. Why he disliked her, Amy didn't know. Try as she might, nothing she did would please him.

Over the next few days, Amy became swamped in departmental paperwork. Everyone thought that all police work was glamourous, but paperwork was something to which no law enforcement person ever got accustomed. She tried to take her mind off what would happen next week by immersing herself in her work. At four-thirty one evening, after punching in her hours at the desk, she grabbed her briefcase and headed out to her car.

Driving home, she listened to the police band to hear what was happening in the area. From out of nowhere, a speeding car screeched around the corner, followed by an RCMP car in hot pursuit. Amy noticed as they sped by that one of the men in the retreating vehicle, the one on the passenger's side, was slouched down in his seat. Amy turned up the police radio and heard Sergeant Miller shout over the air, "In pursuit of a suspect's vehicle, license number AFS-247. Driver is thought to be a suspect in the robbery of the Esso gas station on the Trans-Canada Highway. The male occupant is armed, I repeat, the suspect is armed! I'm now just passing Tim Hortons on Manitoba Drive, heading into Clarenville. Request backup to assist in apprehension of suspect involved."

Amy questioned herself on following them. She was still on suspension, after all, and knew she should not get involved in outside police work until her inquiry was concluded, but decided to follow and see if there was anything she could do to help. Suspended or not, she was still a police officer!

She followed the unit in pursuit of the suspects, but they quickly pulled ahead of her at high speed. She kept track on the police band radio and soon had their location. Sergeant

Miller had trapped the suspect in a cul-de-sac at a new land development about a mile away. Amy decided to go to the back of the area and see if she could be of any help.

A few moments later, she stopped her car on a small hillside and looked down at the scene below her. Sergeant Miller was standing by his car door and shouting at the suspect to exit his car, to throw down any weapon he had, and to lie down on the pavement. Looking from Sergeant Miller to the suspect's vehicle, she now knew why the second suspect, in the passenger seat, had stayed low in his seat. Miller didn't know he was there. As the car door opened from the driver's side of the pursued vehicle, the driver threw his hands in the air to surrender to Sergeant Miller. Meanwhile, the other suspect, who had been crouched down in his seat, had slipped out the passenger door and was crawling on his hands and knees along the side of the car, unnoticed by Sergeant Miller. Amy knew that she was too far away to shout and warn him, and to do so would distract him.

Making her way down the hill, Amy kept the hidden suspect in her sights at all times. She was within fifty feet of him when he sprung up and pointed his gun at Sergeant Miller. Now, only a few feet away, Amy ran as fast as she could toward the man and threw herself at him, blindsiding him and causing the gun to misfire. The man hit the side of the car with an impact that knocked him to the ground, and the gun fell out of his hand. Amy slammed into the rear car door, but managed to deflect any punishment to herself with her arm. The gunman slumped to the pavement, unconscious, as Amy lay stunned and stretched out on the side of the road.

In a matter of minutes, there were a half-dozen police cars converging on scene in the cul-de-sac. Amy was helped to her feet by one of the responding officers. Miller looked at her for a long time from beyond the patrol cars. After the two suspects were cuffed and put in a police car, Amy told one officer that she would drop by the station later and give her statement. Still looking at Sergeant Miller, she turned and walked back to her car. She then realized what she had done, and started to shake. It was a feeling of relief, euphoria, and trepidation all rolled into one. All she could think about now was the reprimand sure to come from Captain Murphy.

She was at home that evening, savouring a fresh shot of whisky, when the doorbell rang. When she opened the door, she stood looking at Sergeant Miller. He asked if he could come in, and Amy nodded. He walked into the living room and sat down, but it was several minutes before he was able to look in her direction. It was the first time she had ever seen Officer Miller like this, weary and shy. He bowed his head for a brief moment and again looked at her. When he spoke, it was in a tone of sadness that Amy had never heard from him or any other police officer before.

"Officer Young, twelve years ago, while I was stationed in

LISA IVANY and ROBERT HUNT

Ontario, I shot and nearly killed a person in a domestic dispute similar to the one we were called out on a few days ago. It happened because I mistook the information given to me by a female police officer before the altercation took place and shots were fired. The officer said she thought the suspect was armed when he wasn't. In the confusion, I took it that he was and fired at him. When we checked him after the shooting, it was found that he had no weapon. Thanks be to God that he didn't die. The inquiry into the shooting exonerated me, but I still blamed the female officer for the mistake that led up to it. All these years I hated working with women on the force. Now, through my stubbornness, I see how wrong I was about what happened to you. I contacted the officer in Ontario and gave her my apology, and now I would like to offer that same apology to you."

Miller stared down at the floor for a second before continuing, "I didn't know there was another suspect in that car. If it were not for you today, I would probably be dead." He looked at Amy with sincerity in his eyes. "Can you please find it in your heart to not only forgive the way I have treated you over the past few years, but to forgive me for not having the common sense to commend you on being the fine police officer that you really are? I've spoken to Captain Murphy and told him what I am telling you now, that you did not cross the tube in that house the other day. I have asked him to recommend you for a promotion because of your heroics at the scene and to drop all charges."

He paused a second before looking straight at Amy. "Lastly, I want you to know, Officer Young, that I will never again treat you with disrespect. I do hope we can start new as friends in our relationship as police officers and as professionals. That is all I have to say. Thank you for your time."

He stood up and walked to the door. Amy followed him to the door and watched as he got in his car.

"Sergeant Miller!"

Miller looked back at her.

"Call me Amy."

Officer Miller smiled and said, "Then I guess I'll see you at the office tomorrow, Amy."

Silencing the Demons

LISA IVANY

Cole Ryder paced back and forth across the cement floor of the garage, brushing his fingers repeatedly through his straight, shoulder-length black hair. He enjoyed working here at his uncle Joe's gas station in Labrador City. After graduating from high school ten years ago, Cole's sole ambition was to help his uncle run the business, and he never once regretted it, even now in early autumn when business was slow after the summer tourist season.

His dark brown eyes creased in agitation beneath black brows, partially clouded by thick, square-framed spectacles. Below a thin wisp of a moustache, his lips curled into a snarl as his mind contemplated his dilemma.

He had received word that his father was visiting Lab City for a few days and wanted a reunion with his son. Cole wanted nothing to do with him. Just knowing he would be returning after all these years brought flashbacks of a very painful youth for Cole, one he had tried hard to forget. The physical scars had healed, the broken bones had mended, but the emotional turmoil from the physical abuse suffered at his father's hands still haunted him. Frequent headaches, nausea, and cold sweats still invaded his life, and the demons in his mind could not be silenced.

Cole Ryder's mother had died in childbirth. While the infant boy was drawing his first breath, his mother drew her last and left her husband, Greg, with a newborn son to raise on his own. He obviously wasn't up to the task, and Cole realized early on that his father blamed him for his mother's death. The verbal attacks brought this to light when Greg had been drinking heavily, which was quite often. The tongue-lashings were enough to destroy Cole's self-esteem, but they would also be accompanied by beatings severe enough to land him in hospital. Of course, on each admission he'd give a story such as falling down the stairs or running into a door.

Cole was thirteen when he moved in with his uncle Joe, after his father was charged with assaulting a man in a local pub. He was later found guilty and sent to prison in another province. Although he had been released several years ago, Greg Ryder had never returned home, and Cole wondered why he was coming back now.

"Hey, what's up, man?" a voice spoke, startling him from his musings and interrupting his brisk pacing habit.

"Darcy! Don't sneak up on me like that!" Cole snapped.

"What's bugging you?" Blair asked, stepping out from behind Darcy.

"You guys should know."

"Yeah, Blair," Darcy said, "have you forgotten who's about to waltz back into Cole's life?"

"Sorry, Cole. I forgot about that," Blair apologized.

Darcy lit a cigarette and inhaled deeply. On exhaling, the smoke billowed in thick clouds above the trio in the garage, initiating an episode of coughing from Cole. He was allergic to smoke, and, even though Darcy knew this, he continued to smoke in Cole's presence. *He is so annoying*, Cole thought.

"Well, have you given any thought to what I suggested?" Darcy asked.

"Forget it," Cole answered.

"What are you talking about?" Blair asked.

"I told Cole he should snuff out his old man when he comes to visit. All Cole has to do is get his father to visit him at night after the shop is closed, grab Joe's pistol under the till, then shoot the idiot. He could tell the cops he thought his father was a burglar."

"Are you crazy, Darcy?" Blair said.

"You two are such cowards!" Darcy exclaimed. "Maybe I'll just do it myself."

Sucking in the last draw of his cigarette, Darcy crushed it under his foot onto the cement floor. He strode from the garage with Blair chasing his heels. Before the door closed behind them, Cole thought he heard Darcy say, "Death to the father or death to the son."

He often wondered what life would be like without Darcy and Blair. Although Darcy was the obvious leader of their group, Blair's spineless behaviour mimicked Cole's own. He owed Darcy a lot, though. He had been with Cole and Blair since they were children and came to their aid on many occasions. Nobody went up against Darcy, and if you were his friend, you were safe by association. Darcy and Blair had steadfastly supported him during all his years of physical and emotional abuse.

As a youth, Cole was prone to an occasional headache, usually when his father's verbal assaults went longer and louder than usual. These headaches subsided after Greg Ryder's incarceration, but since Cole had heard of his father's release from prison, they returned in a chronic, unrelenting manner. They had become so disabling that Cole was completely incapable of working if one came on.

Uncle Joe had converted the upstairs storage room into a bedroom where Cole could go and lie down if he felt a headache come on during his shift. Lately, the headaches would persist into the evening and Cole would take a sedative and stay the night. However, the demons inside his head would not let him rest.

Cole zipped up his navy windbreaker before leaving for his appointment with Dr. Nolan. The sun was shining this afternoon, but the autumn air was a little chilly. He grabbed his motorcycle helmet from the shelf and left the garage.

"Hey, Cole!" a voice called from one of the gas pumps. "Wait a minute."

"What's up, Uncle Joe?"

The short, hefty man with receding grey hair left the car he was pumping gas into and quickly walked to his nephew. His normally jovial expression was now one of concern.

"I had a call a little while ago from your father. He wants to come by and see you this evening, but I wasn't sure what to tell him," Joe stated. "If you don't want to see him alone, I can join you."

"I have no wish to see him," Cole responded. He pulled the burgundy helmet over his head, mounted his motorcycle, and rode away. At the end of the parking lot, he stopped and lifted his visor. "Tell him I'll see him here at the garage tonight after I close up," he yelled. "I'd prefer to see him alone, Uncle Joe, if that's okay with you."

His uncle nodded his compliance and said, "I'll call and let him know."

Cole didn't know why he gave in to seeing the man who had destroyed his youth and who still troubled his mind. Maybe he wanted to confront his father and perhaps get an apology from him, but what good would that do now? Perhaps Darcy's plan of ridding the world of Greg Ryder wasn't such a bad idea.

Painted on the waiting room door in gold lettering was "Dr. Ian Nolan, Psychiatrist." Cole entered the familiar area, the one he had been visiting for many years even before the voices started. It was Dr. Nolan who had diagnosed Cole with major depression and multiple personality disorder. He had been receiving treatment since his teenage years and, although he still exhibited symptoms, many of the personalities had vanished with extensive psychotherapy. He had been tried on various antidepressants over the years, but had only achieved minimal success.

Cole scanned the waiting room and noticed that it was filled. He came to the conclusion that the good doctor must be running at least a couple of hours behind. An hour ticked by painstakingly slowly, with only one patient called in, so Cole left the clinic. Ordinarily he would have waited, but his agitation at the upcoming reunion with his father threw him into a tailspin. He couldn't sit still another moment.

After locking up the garage for the night, Cole went upstairs to his room to await his father's arrival. Darcy and Blair had appeared just before Cole turned out the lights and convinced him to retrieve the gun. They joined him in his room for moral support. Cole held the weapon in his hand, checked to see that it was fully loaded, and nervously laid it on the nightstand.

"I can't go through with this," Cole remarked.

"Of course you can," Darcy insisted. "You know it's the only way to be free of him."

"No," Cole snapped. "This would make me even worse than he is."

"I knew you'd chicken out!" Darcy roared. "You should have a yellow stripe running down your back!"

"Hey, guys. Calm down," Blair interjected.

"Stay out of this! You're just as yellow as he is!" Darcy yelled. Snatching the gun, he snarled, "I'm sick of hanging around with losers. Greg Ryder is not the one who needs to die, Cole, it's you!"

Darcy jabbed the end of the pistol forcefully under Cole's chin, snapping his head back with the sudden thrust. Terror flooded Cole's eyes as he realized his assailant had no intention of letting go. Darcy emitted a maniacal laugh that would have sent a chill through the devil himself.

He pulled back the hammer until it clicked. Just one tug with his index finger and it would be lights out for Cole.

"You're making a big mistake," Cole pleaded. "Just put the gun down and we'll talk about it."

"That's all you ever want to do. You think talking is going to help, but it doesn't, Cole!" Darcy barked. "You've been talking to that shrink of yours, and where has it gotten you?"

"We've come a long way with Dr. Nolan, and we're getting a little better every day."

"You're so naive! You think he's great just because he helped eliminate Derek, Scott, and Bernie. They were only weak personalities that would have disappeared in time anyway," Darcy continued. "You'll probably get rid of this pansy, Blair, eventually too, but I'll always be around because, like it or not, you need me. You're too weak to stand on your own."

Realizing the truth in Darcy's words, Cole no longer feared the weapon's discharge. In fact, he longed for it. He knew his father's death would not give him the freedom he sought. The demons were inside his own head in the personalities of Darcy and Blair, and though he could not live with them, he knew he couldn't live without them either. Suddenly, the road before him seemed insurmountable and his depression plummeted to rock bottom.

Goading Darcy into the action he wanted, Cole spat out, "You're wrong. I led you to believe you were in charge, but I was pulling your strings all along. You're nothing without me."

"You just signed your death sentence, moron!"

Darcy pulled the trigger, setting off an explosion of gunfire, followed by a heavy thump as Cole hit the floor. The point of impact was a little off-centre, beneath his chin, shattering his mandible and exiting just above his left eye. He felt a searing pain along the left side of his face and forehead, but the voices were gone. Finally, they lay silent.

The door flew open and slammed against the wall. *That must be my father*, Cole thought. While he lay with his head in a hot pool of scarlet liquid, the man he had feared and despised all his life walked through the doorway. But Cole no longer felt angry.

He knew his death would be called a suicide, but was it

really? Sure, his fingerprints were on the weapon and it was fired with his hand, but Cole and Blair knew that Darcy was the one who had pulled the trigger. It really didn't matter to Cole anymore, because his demons were now silent. As he closed his eyes for the last time, he knew he was free at last.

Stay With Me

ROBERT HUNT

Grant Farrell loved the hot days of summer, but this year he could not wait for it to be over. The happiness the season brought eluded him this year, he thought as he navigated LeMarchant Road traffic on his way to St. Clare's Mercy Hospital. He reminisced of the many wonderful summers he and his wife had spent together. They had three children, who were now married with families of their own. Grant and Rita spent the best part of their forty-seven years of marriage with their children and grandchildren.

But this year was different. Grant, now sixty-seven, and Rita, at sixty-five, had just started to enjoy retirement when Rita's problems began. She started feeling sick early last November, having come down with a strange virus that robbed her of her strength. Within weeks, Grant had to help her in and out of bed. She also needed help dressing and doing all the other little everyday things she could no longer do on her own. The doctors were confident the sickness would eventually go away, but Rita's health continued to decline.

Then, after many tests and trips to the hospital, they were told that Rita had Alzheimer's disease. A few months later, Rita suffered a brain hemorrhage. Now, two years later, Grant found himself virtually living at the hospital. Rita, when she remembered things, was always in an upbeat mood during his visits, and he knew that it was her courage in handling her disease that kept him strong.

All through their marriage, Grant and Rita had been very close. Wherever you saw one, you saw the other; they were inseparable. Their friends envied their devotion to each other. They showered love on their children and grandchildren, and they had a way of touching the hearts of everyone who knew them. They were the perfect couple. Grant was devastated when he learned that his wife's failing health would be her end, and secretly he wished he could trade places with her.

Grant had gotten into the habit of bringing along a tape recorder when he visited Rita. He had started recording his conversations with her the first few days after she had been admitted. In his heart he felt it was important for him to record what was being said by them both. A lot of it did not make sense because Rita's Alzheimer's was in the advanced

AT HEART

stages, and she drifted off on many topics. It would be only a matter of time, Grant knew, before he would no longer be able to hear her voice, and he wanted something to remember her by. The doctors at St. Clare's said that her time was now limited to a matter of months, maybe weeks.

Grant entered the hospital's elevator and got off on the third floor. He walked into Rita's room and glanced down at her in the bed. She was sound asleep, and looked so peaceful that he contented himself with just watching her for a while. He gently stroked her hand and, though asleep, her fingers instinctively curled around his.

"What can I do for you, my darling? For so many years we have been there for each other, through the good times and the bad, and now I feel so helpless. What can I do for you?"

Grant laid his head on the bed next to Rita's hand and within minutes fell into a deep sleep. He dreamed that her hand was resting gently on his head. He looked up, and she was smiling down, her eyes open and clear of the confusion that had plagued them for so long.

"Grant, I know that you are with me, so I am not worried. You have watched over me for most of my life, and now it is time for you to take care of yourself. I must leave you soon. You are a good man, you have been a wonderful husband, and I will love you always."

Rita smiled again, and Grant awakened, shaking his head in amazement at the clarity of his dream. Rita's voice, the touch of her hand, even the smells of the hospital room had seemed so real! But he knew the dream for what it was. Rita had slipped into a coma several weeks ago; there was no way she could have spoken to him. An hour later, he kissed his wife on the forehead and said good night.

On the way out of the hospital, Grant asked the nurses to notify him if there was any change in Rita's condition. On the way home, he thought about what to do when she was gone. How could he possibly go on without her? They lived for each other. All he had was a few jumbled words on a tape recorder.

At that moment, after the dozens of hospital visits, the realization that his wife was leaving him overwhelmed Grant. He pulled into a vacant lot, turned off the car's engine, and cried. After some time, his sobs lessened, and he fumbled for his keys. His hand closed around the tape recorder in his pocket. He sighed, laid it on the seat next to him, and turned it on.

"Grant, I know that you are with me."

The hairs on the back of Grant's neck stood up. He broke out in a cold sweat. His heart thumping rapidly, he hit the stop button and just stared at the tape recorder. *That's impossible!* His mind screamed. Trying to control his breathing, he slowly reached for the device and hit the rewind button. When the tape stopped spinning, he pressed Play again. And there it was: Rita's rich, clear voice spilled out of the tape recorder, repeating what she had said in Grant's dream!

AT HEART

Grant played the tape again and again. *My God,* he thought. He raced home, hopped out of the car, and ran across the road to his brother's house. Calvin met him at the door, and Grant quickly told him what had just happened in the hospital and on his way home. Calvin invited him in and watched as his brother took out the tape recorder. Grant hit the Play button, and the two men strained their ears when the faint hiss of a recording began. But there was nothing else. Grant looked up at his brother, then rewound the tape and set it to play again. Again, no sound but that faint hiss came out.

Grant stared at his brother for a long moment. "Calvin, I swear to you that Rita's voice came out of that recorder on the way from the hospital. I don't know what's happening."

"I'm sure it did, Grant, but maybe you're the only one who can hear it. You've been under a lot of pressure lately because of Rita's illness. Maybe you imagined it."

Calvin thought his brother was overreacting, and maybe he was right. Grant had not been sleeping well lately, and imagined he heard Rita's voice talking to him at night while he was tossing and turning.

Grant took the recorder back to his house and laid it on the kitchen table. *I couldn't have heard her voice. I must be going crazy.* He looked at the recorder, his hand hovering above the control buttons for. He hit Play.

"Grant, I know that you are with me."

My God, what is happening here? Am I going mad?

He rewound it and listened to the tape as if he were hypnotized. This time letting it play through.

"... I will love you always."

Then there was silence. Grant reached to shut off the recorder, when Rita's voice spoke again.

"Grant, do not be afraid. Somehow God has given me a way to communicate with you through this recorder, but you are the only one who can hear me. I feel like I am floating in some kind of space, and you are the only one I can speak to. Do not be afraid. I will speak with you again tonight."

Grant couldn't believe what he was hearing. He quickly showered and changed his clothes. At 5:00 that evening, he left for the hospital again. He had been feeling very fatigued lately, the strain of living at the hospital having taken its toll, but he didn't care. Rita was his life, and he was going to spend as much time with her as he could before the end.

When he got to her room, Grant took the tape recorder out of his pocket, pressed Record, and sat beside the bed. Rita, of course, was still asleep. He laid his hand on hers and rested his head on the blanket, just as he had before. In a few minutes, he too was fast asleep.

"Grant, we have been given a gift by the grace of God," Rita said to him in his sleep, "and we only have this last conversation to use it. You see, I have been told that I will be

AT HEART

leaving in a short while to be with Him. I was told that I could talk to you once more before that happens. I want you to know that I have always loved you and will see you again soon. Please take care of yourself, and remember, I will always be with you."

This time, Grant found he could respond. "Rita, I have never loved anyone as I have loved you. Although you will be gone, we will never be apart. I will love you always."

At 5:30, Nurse Chambers entered the room and noticed Mr. Farrell asleep at his wife's side. She decided to let him sleep; she knew he spent a lot of time at the hospital, and the two of them looked so peaceful. Closing the door softly behind her, she resumed her duties. At 7:00, she returned to give Rita Farrell her medication. She went to the bedside and gave Mr. Farrell a gentle tap on the shoulder to wake him. He did not stir. Again she tapped him, and still no response. Alarmed, Nurse Chambers called a code blue and the team arrived immediately. One doctor checked Grant's vitals while another moved over to check on Rita.

Because Rita's chart contained a Do Not Resuscitate order, they let her slip away, freeing from her pain at last. Meanwhile, the doctor who had been checking Grant's vitals finally looked up, shaking his head.

"My, oh my," Dr. Williams said. "It seems that Mr. Farrell passed away at the same time his wife did."

Nurse Chambers noticed a tape recorder under Grant's arm. "Dr. Williams, look at this."

The doctor took the device from beneath Grant's arm and rewound the spent tape. He laid it on the lunch cart and hit Play.

"My sweet wife," Grant Farrell's voice said, "I know now that I cannot bear to go on without you. I am asking God to please take me with you when you leave. Life, to me, will be nothing if I cannot spend it with you on this earth."

The hospital staff listened in shock, some in tears, as Rita, who had been in a coma, spoke to her husband.

"Grant, I was willing to leave this earth without you, as it was God's will that I do so because my time was up. I wish you could come with me, but we have no control over that. Our fate is in God's Hands."

There was a short pause, then Grant's voice continued. "I have prayed many times since your illness to join you when you go. Life means nothing to me without you." Nurse Chambers and the other members of the medical team heard him sigh. "Please, God, if you can't let Rita stay with me, then please take me with her."

Dr. Williams looked around the room at the nursing staff, slowly reached across the table, and turned off the tape recorder.

Stranger Behind the Mask

LISA IVANY

Corinna Timmons stood before the full-length mirror in her bedroom and appraised herself. Dressed as a geisha, she grinned at the youthful reflection gazing back at her. In a few weeks she would turn thirty, however, in this outfit she could easily pass for a teenager. Surely everyone at the Halloween party would be guessing at the identity of the lovely young woman.

Corinna wore a long, flowered, pink and lilac kimono bound at the waist by a wide sash of burgundy. The long sleeves were tapered at the wrists in a triangular fashion, with gold embroidered dragons spiralling to her shoulders. Thick white powder covered her face, with a generous dab of cherry lipstick, and thick black mascara accentuating large chocolate eyes.

Without warning, a ninja warrior, clad in black satin shirt, trousers, and head mask sprang into her doorway and dropped to a crouched position. He raised his arms to chest level and made circular motions with his hands, as though readying for an attack. Corinna didn't flinch. After being engaged to Chad Holden for the last two years, she knew his proclivity for practical jokes and had been anticipating this. Although his face was completely covered, his head and shoulders drooped significantly, like those of a sullen child. She laughed at his obvious disappointment in not startling her.

Rebounding, he remarked, "You look awesome!"

"You're not so bad yourself. Especially with your face covered."

"I guess you'll be walking to Dana's party alone then," Chad countered.

"You know I think you're handsome with or without the mask." Corinna planted a kiss on his black satin cheek to emphasize the point.

He backed away and said, "You're just trying to soften me up for a ride."

"Did it work?"

"You know I can't resist a Japanese lady in distress," he replied before bending from the waist in an exaggerated bow of gallantry.

Although Dana Fifield lived just a short distance down

the road, they drove instead of walking, due to the inclement weather. The wind showed its discontent, with eerie, high-pitched squeals, sending a shiver down Corinna's spine. It was an appropriate setting for Halloween and she was a little uneasy, as though expecting a ghost or some other creepy creature to spring out from the darkness. An audible sigh escaped her lips when they pulled into the car-filled lot next to the Fifield residence.

The old Victorian home, which was bright and welcoming during the day, was now decorated in sinister style for the occasion. All the windows were covered in black, and huge blankets of artificial cobwebs covered the veranda. The only light in the area came from the jack-o'-lanterns lining the driveway and steps.

Dressed as Cleopatra, Dana greeted her guests at the door and ushered them into the living room, which had been converted into a dance hall. The party was in full swing, and Corinna and Chad surveyed the dancers on the floor. They ranged from friendly Little Bo Peep and Red Riding Hood to darker fiends such as Dracula and the Grim Reaper.

Satisfied they had discovered the identities of all the costumed guests, they sat down for a drink before joining the dancers. It was Chad's turn to be the designated driver tonight, so he would be relegated to drinking cola. Corinna was under no such restrictions and started the night off with a glass of sangria.

Many heads turned to stare at the geisha throughout the

night, to admire the detailing of her costume, and also to try and figure out who she was. This caused Corinna to giggle, especially since most of these people were her close friends. She wasn't discovered until after midnight, when Chad could suffer the heat no longer and removed his mask. Once his face was revealed, it was obvious who his partner was.

Several dances and several sangrias later, Corinna leaned against a wall as a wave of dizziness washed over her.

She heard a voice ask, "Are you all right?"

Corinna recognized Keith Thompson, who was not wearing a costume, and replied, "I'm fine."

"You don't look fine. Would you like a ride home?"

"No thanks. Chad will drive me." The thought of going anywhere with Keith made Corinna's skin crawl. She felt there was something sinister about the way he always looked at her. It was as though he were trying to steal a piece of her soul.

She spied Chad across the room with his friends and moved over to him, saying, "I'm feeling a little queasy. Would you mind taking me home?"

"Take you home, already?" Chad exclaimed. "But this is the best party we've been to in ages, and all the guys from the hockey team are here!"

"I'm sorry, Chad, but I think I'm going to be sick."

"I told you to take it easy on the drinks, but you never listen."

"Okay, I'll never have another sangria as long as I live," Corinna vowed. "Now, please take me home."

AT HEART

"I'll get Brent to give you a drive. He said he's leaving soon anyway because his Grim Reaper costume is acting as a female repellent. Just give me a minute to track him down." Corinna gave him a dirty look, threw her hands in the air, and stormed out of the house.

Outside, she shivered in the chill night air and hugged herself, remembering the jacket left inside. "Well, I'm not going back in there," she muttered angrily.

Corinna shivered again, then hurried down the dark street. She flinched when a car pulled up beside her, then relaxed when she saw it was only Brent, still in his Grim Reaper costume.

"You're just in time," she said. "Another minute and I'd have been frozen stiff."

Feeling the warmth of the car's heater circulating around her body, Corinna relaxed into the comfort of the seat and closed her eyes. She couldn't believe Chad would stay at the party instead of taking her home when she wasn't feeling well. He would certainly get a piece of her mind tomorrow. That is, if she decided to talk to him at all.

The car stopped, and, in her drunken state, Corinna felt arms encircling her shoulders and pulling her down on the seat. She opened her eyes to see Brent had stopped on one of the abandoned gravel roads that led from the highway at the end of Valleyfield. From her brief glance, it looked like the lane everyone referred to as Haunted Hollow, a place they avoided after dark. A hand grappled with the buttons on her costume, undoing them in a hurried fashion.

Corinna shrieked, "Brent Pickett, what do you think you're doing?"

"Who's Brent?" whispered the voice from behind the mask.

She immediately came to her senses and realized the severity of her situation. She was on a deserted road late at night with a stranger forcing his unwanted attentions upon her. Wriggling free of his arms, she pushed against his chest to free herself, but he was much stronger. He pulled her down farther upon the seat so they were both fully reclined, with his entire weight on top of her. Corinna started to scream.

"You can scream as loud as you like, but no one will hear you."

The sound of his voice was familiar, but Corinna couldn't place it. She tried grasping his mask to reveal his identity, but he grabbed her hand and pinned it behind her. He held her other hand in a viselike grip, knowing her strength was no match for his own.

The wind howled through the dark night. Black, heavy-limbed trees waved in the night's breeze, as though applauding her assailant.

The Reaper said, "Don't you know, in Japan, geishas are supposed to please their men?"

"Well," replied Corinna through clenched teeth, "We're not in Japan."

The stranger chuckled at her retort and pulled her dress

up to her waist, purposely brushing his hand along her exposed thigh in the process. "You have beautiful legs," he murmured, gliding his hand up farther.

He released her struggling hand and made to remove his own clothing. That was all the time Corinna needed to extract one of the long, sharp pins from her hair. She lashed out, and the needle jabbed the man in the thigh. He screamed and clutched his leg, and Corinna used this opportunity to scramble out of the car.

Panic-stricken, she raced down the gravel road while taking several frightened looks behind to make sure no one was following. She recognized the rocky path now, lined with a thick growth of alders, junipers, and tall bunches of purple wildflowers. Their petals, bent double from the wind, bowed to the narrow road. The wind continued to howl and tossed branches about as though in a devil's dance. She sensed a fluttering motion above her head and wondered if it was bats' wings.

She collided with something solid. The jolt drew a startled scream from her lips, but the scream was cut short when she focused on the ninja. He no longer wore his mask and his expression was one of concern. Corinna leapt into his arms and exclaimed, "Oh Chad, I'm so glad to see you! How did you find me?"

He replied, "After you left, I felt awful about staying without you, so I left too. On my way out, I noticed Brent wasn't wearing his costume. He said Keith had asked to borrow it, and that's when I started to feel uneasy."

"Keith Thompson! That's why his voice was so familiar. But that still doesn't tell me how you found me."

"Actually, it was just a hunch. You see, when Keith and I were younger, we used to go exploring in this area. However, we never came here at night. Keith said he felt as though you could do anything you want in here and no one would ever know."

Corinna started to weep as the full impact of the night's events started to take its toll. As Chad put his arms around her, she whimpered, "I was so scared."

"Everything's okay now," he said.

In the early morning hours, Keith was escorted in handcuffs to the back seat of a squad car. He had fled to the forest's cocoon of darkness when he spotted the flashing red and blue lights, but the officers outran him and quickly apprehended their suspect. Through the window, he pierced Corinna with an icy stare as they pulled away.

"How could I have been so stupid, Chad?"

"What do you mean?"

"I got in the car with him, didn't I?"

"Yes, but you didn't know it was Keith behind the wheel," Chad reasoned.

She grimaced. "I can still feel his hands all over me."

Corinna began to sob again, and when she was done, Chad took her hand in his and said, "Come on. Let me take you home like I should have done in the first place."

Renconciliation

ROBERT HUNT

Many thoughts flooded Brian Campbell's mind as he sat in the car and stared at the split-level home located at 211 Mercury Drive. He could see that it had been recently renovated, with new vinyl siding that made the home look bigger than it really was. Though it was an older home, it seemed to have it's own distinct character.

Brian wondered what lay beyond the front door, and how to choose his words once it opened. It seemed better to let the people inside do the talking and gauge their reaction. He hadn't seen them for years. *Well, no sense sitting here,* he decided. He had been sitting in the car for nearly thirty minutes, and now, with a heavy sigh, stepped from his vehicle onto the street. He had just arrived in Calgary; guilt had brought him there. *Oh, if I could only bring the years back*. He sighed again and walked to the front door.

Brian felt a pang of remorse, and his pace slowed. He again wondered what kind of reception he would get after having walked out on his family. *I should just leave*, he thought, but he knew he couldn't. His life would never be complete if he didn't do now what he had set out to do.

After working in Scarborough, Ontario for ten years, he had recently retired and moved back to Fogo, Newfoundland. The purpose that had brought him back here to Calgary, Alberta, had for several years now seemed the only thing he could do to make peace with himself. Now was not the time for doubts. Brian took a deep breath, let it out, and took his last step toward the home. He knocked lightly on the solid black door. A woman's voice could be heard inside.

"Honey, can you get the door for me? I'm busy in the kitchen."

A male voice answered in agreement. The seconds seemed like an eternity to Brian as he waited. The door opened, and a tall, well-groomed man of about thirty-five answered.

"Yes, may I help you?" the young man asked.

Brian Campbell smiled but looked past him, to catch a glimpse inside at the real reason for the visit.

"Hello, Albert. I wonder if I may step inside for a moment?"

AT HEART

A look of shock replaced Albert's curious expression, and he slowly backed away from the door and into the hallway. He motioned Brian inside and nodded for the older man to take a seat.

"Helen, I think you should come out here for a second."

Helen came out, and immediately her hand went to her mouth. She stared at Brian, speechless. The ticking hall clock sounded loudly in Brian's ears.

"Dad? What brings you here? And how did you know where I lived?"

Brian turned his head in embarrassment and spoke just above a whisper. "Hello, Helen. I was speaking to your mother a few days ago in Fogo and asked her where you were. When she told me, I decided to fly out. I wanted to see you and my grandson. I . . . I know it's been a long time, but I would like to talk to you both . . . if that's okay with you and Albert."

Albert shook his head. "Helen is capable of making her own decisions, Mr. Campbell. If she wants, I'll leave you two alone to talk."

Brian followed Helen in to the living room. His daughter sat and waited for him to speak. He glanced around the room and noticed a picture of a young boy, around eight years old, atop the piano.

"Would this be my grandson, Adam?" he asked.

"Yes it is, Dad," was all Helen could say. Her uneasiness was not lost on Brian as he tried to find the words.

He nodded, and continued to stare at Adam's picture. "Look, I know this is probably not right, to come to see you. I've had no contact with you, your brother, or your mother for many years, but I just had to do this now. For so long I have had trouble trying to cope with the problems in my life, I've come to realize that I need all of you back in it."

Helen gave her father a hard look. "Why, Dad? As you just said, you left us years ago and never made contact with any of us. Why would you want to come see us now? Mom has remarried, and Sean is grown and married with a family, also. As you can see, I have a wonderful home here with Albert. Why should I let you back in our lives after you left us so abruptly? Please, give me one good reason why I should."

Brian looked at his daughter. How beautiful she had grown since he had last seen her. She was as beautiful as her mother.

"You have every reason to hate me," he said softly. "I caused you a lot of pain. Your mother and I had our problems, but I never had any anger toward you or Sean. You have to believe that, Helen."

"Why should I believe you, Dad?" Helen said with tears in her eyes. "If you cared for us as you say you do, why did you wait so long? I'm sorry about the problems that you had in your past, but we had problems, too, in growing up without a father."

"I understand, Helen. If you hate me, if you want me to leave, I will. I just had to try to and make things better with you before I go back to Newfoundland. I know what I've done and I only want one thing. Your forgiveness. All I can say is that I'm truly sorry."

Many emotions surfaced as Helen looked at her estranged father. She was happy with her life here. Still, she felt pity for the man who had abandoned them years ago.

"Dad, I don't hate you. I feel sorry for you and the wasted life you've lived for so many years. Adam is your grandchild, so I have to tell you something."

A tear spilled down one cheek as she continued. "If you had kept in contact with us, you would have known that Adam has been a very sick child. He was born with spina bifida, which has caused a severe curvature of his spine. He is, at this moment, still in the Calgary Children's Hospital; he's been in and out of hospitals since he was two years old. His condition is very painful, and sometimes he has difficulty walking."

Brian knew that Helen was not telling him this to make him feel guilty; it was just very hard for her to deal with her son's condition.

"Your mother never told me about Adam's condition. I guess she wanted you to tell me. Please, may I go see him?"

"Regardless of what has happened in your life," Helen said, "he is still your grandson. We are going to see him this evening. If you want, you can meet us there at seven."

Brian knew that all would not be forgiven quickly. He hadn't been a father to Helen when she needed one. He nodded, knowing that he had to start somewhere.

Brian left Helen's house and immediately went to the Calgary Children's Hospital. His intention was to visit Adam's doctor to determine the extent of his grandson's condition. He made inquiries, and was introduced to Dr. Rideout, a physician specializing in spinal cord conditions in children. Brian told him that Adam was his grandson and asked what he could do for him. Dr. Rideout told him that Adam was born with a defect that bent his spine into a curve and that it would probably not straighten itself out until he had a spinal fusion. This procedure was done every day in Calgary, but, due to a rare anomaly in Adam's case, his could not be done in Canada. It was a risky surgery, one which had only been attempted a few times by Dr. Paul Hartley, a renowned spina bifida specialist in Texas. Dr. Rideout confided in Brian that Adam's parents could not afford to have it done. Brian asked him what the total cost would be.

The doctor replied, "He would have to spend at least two months in hospital after the operation for proper rehabilitation, so one of his parents would have to be there with him. That would be an additional cost, plus the procedure itself. Where there is no medicare in the United States, it would probably be in the range of about $250,000."

Brian said, "Dr. Rideout, I am a very rich man. I made my money a few years ago in Ontario, investing in a business and the stock market. I did very well. I have the money to help Adam, but I have been estranged from my family for years, and I don't know if my daughter will accept my help."

He took a deep breath. "Doctor, I found out that I only have a short time to live. I would like to donate all the money needed for Adam's surgery and recuperation. Money is no object. However, I would like you to inform his parents that it was an anonymous donation, because I'm not sure they would accept it from me."

Dr. Rideout nodded. "Is it cancer?"

"It doesn't matter, Doctor. I've seen several specialists, and all gave me the same diagnosis; it's terminal. So, for once in my life, I am going to do the right thing and take care of someone else, instead of myself. Please say you will help me."

The doctor agreed and said he could accept the donation anonymously. He asked Brian if he wished to see Adam. At first Brian hesitated, but the doctor convinced him to go into the rehabilitation room and observe his grandson. Brian followed Dr. Rideout down several corridors and into a room with a large window overlooking a large gymnasium. Inside the gymnasium, young people with disabilities were being treated. Dr. Rideout pointed through the glass at a freckle-faced eight-year-old boy who was laughing at his trainer as they threw a ball back and forth. Brian saw how difficult it was for Adam to manoeuvre his small frame to retrieve the ball when it came his way. Brian was moved, and as he watched the grandson he never knew, he was overcome with feelings of love and adoration. He made peace with himself then, and tears slid down his face; he forgave himself for the things he had done, and vowed that he would put to good use every second of his life that he had left.

Brian lingered at the hospital a little longer, then went back to his hotel. He showered, and as the warm, cleansing water hit him, he began to feel like a new man. His own troubled childhood, the beatings he had endured growing up, all of these bitter memories to which he had clung for so long, lifted from him. They had no control over him now, and his life was finally his to live. His children, and Adam, would no longer be made victims of Brian's own tragic upbringing.

He headed back to the hospital, where Helen and Albert met him at the entrance. He didn't know how he would react when he saw Adam again; he expected it would be strange speaking to his grandson for the first time. They arrived on the second floor shortly, and Brian felt like he was floating as he left the elevator. As they entered his grandson's room, it seemed he was in a different world.

"Hello, Adam . . . I'm your poppy," was all Brian could manage.

"Hi, Poppy," said Adam, wide-eyed. "What took you so long to visit me?" In that instant, Brian's heart melted. He took his grandson's small hand in his own.

He looked at Helen and Albert before speaking again. "Forgive me, Adam, for I have been away for such a long time, and it's only now that I've returned. If you will let me, and if it is okay with your mom and dad, I would like to make up for some of the time I have missed with you."

AT HEART

Brian looked at Helen and Albert, then sat beside Adam's bed. Grandfather and grandson spent the next two hours talking like old friends who hadn't seen each other in years. When visiting hours were over, he left Adam's room. As he walked down the hallway, he eyed a statue of St. Jude, whose eyes seemed to be following him to the elevator. Maybe it was a trick of the light, but Brian fancied he saw the statue nodding, as if in approval of what had just happened.

The next day, Brian requested another audience with Dr. Rideout. When he finished his consultation with the doctor, he returned to his hotel room and phoned the law offices of Pearce, Small & Young, a small firm he dealt with back home.

"Good morning. How may I direct your call?" the secretary answered. "This is Brian Campbell. I wish to speak to Mr. Hiram Young, please."

"One moment, Mr. Campbell. I'll get him for you."

After a few moments, Hiram Young came on the line.

"Good morning, Brian. How are you?"

"Hiram, my good friend, I would like you to do something for me. I want you to take $500,000 dollars of my money and put it in a fund for my grandson, Adam Parks, here at Calgary Children's Hospital. Adam is to have a spinal operation in Houston, Texas. I will have his physician, Dr. Rideout, send you the details about how to wire the money for Adam's operation. I also want $4,000,000 dollars, two million dollars each, to be put into two separate checking accounts for my two children, Sean and Helen. The remaining $2,200,000 I wish to leave to my ex-wife, Paula. Do you understand my instructions?"

"Why, yes, Brian. They will be carried out immediately upon receiving your papers and according to your wishes. But may I ask why you are taking nearly all of your money from the bank? What about your business? "

Brian smiled. "That's where you come in. You see, Hiram, all my life I have been consumed by a desire to make money on the backs of so many other people. I fought my way to the top in the business world. Once I got there, I realized that there is no top. It took the beauty of an eight-year-old boy to make me realize how foolish it all was, and now I see that there are more important things in this life than money and power. That boy is in a hospital bed waiting for me this very minute."

"Brian, this is so sudden," Hiram gushed. "Are you sure of this? Would you like some time to think about what you are asking me to do?"

Brian cut him off. "Hiram, I've never been so sure of anything in my entire life as I am about this. Please do what I will instruct you to do in my letters, and take care of yourself. Goodbye, my friend."

Brian laid the phone down, effectively ending the conversation. He put on his coat and walked the short distance back to the hospital.

AT HEART

Brian Campbell passed away fourteen months after his first visit to the Calgary Children's Hospital, but lived long enough to see Adam walk and his disability corrected. Adam received his operation in Texas, and before turning ten, walked without help from his crutches. Before Brian died, he reconciled with his two children and his ex-wife. They lived, with the help of his money, the kind of life he could not give them while he was alive, but they were grateful for his kindness in the end.

Rendezvous With Destiny

LISA IVANY

"*I can't believe you're* cancelling my birthday plans to go golfing with your brother," I scolded.

"But, Sandy, I'm not cancelling anything. I'm just postponing our plans for one day," Cameron pleaded. "We can go out to dinner and take in a movie tomorrow night. If you're lucky, you might even convince me to get on the dance floor at Legends afterwards."

"*Today* is my birthday, not tomorrow, and it's not every day a person turns forty. I know I said I didn't want a big party for my birthday, but I was looking forward to going out tonight and meeting up with the gang for drinks later on," I responded irritably. Legends was our favourite pub in Gander, and I knew our friends would be there tonight because it was their usual hangout on Friday nights for happy hour. I thought it would cheer me up because I dreaded turning forty. I felt so old!

Very rarely did we argue, but Cameron and I had only been married a few months and were still getting used to the idea of co-habiting. Even being called Mrs. Ford was quite an adjustment. Although we had known each other since childhood, we only started dating two years ago, after we'd ended up working together at Cobb's Pond.

It was during Gander's Festival of Flight celebration, our annual civic holiday. Normally, the pond is a peaceful place, used mostly by picnickers or people taking advantage of the boardwalk that circles the water. However, for one day a year, it is the hub of commotion for the Gander Day holiday, with rows of concession booths lining the road. Throngs of spectators cover the large grassy field, watching either the musical performances at the far end of the pond or the Search and Rescue demonstrations over the water.

Cameron and I had volunteered to work in the first aid tent and were paired together for most of the morning. After several hours of attending to minor incidents and a few cases of mild sunstroke, we were partnered again for a shift in the canteen. Over the course of the day, we came to discover we had a lot in common. By the time the Gander Day fireworks concluded that night, we knew we had started some fireworks of our own.

But that was the furthest thing from my mind now as I

fumed over my husband's thoughtlessness. I worked as a nurse and Cameron as an air traffic controller, frequently working opposite shifts to each other with rare weekends off together. Here it was, a Friday, my fortieth birthday, and we were both lucky enough to have the weekend off . . . but the numbskull would rather spend it with his brother!

"Honey, Duncan goes back to Wabush tomorrow," Cameron pressed, "and the only tee-off time we could get was for 5:30 this evening."

"Fine! Go ahead and enjoy your day on the golf course," I pouted. "I'll find something to do."

"Great! I knew you'd understand, sweetie."

I realized my self-pity act was lost on Cameron as he sprinted to the garage with his golf clubs in tow and boarded the van. Within seconds the engine whirred and he was off to his parents' home to pick up his brother. Duncan lived in Wabush and came home about four times a year to visit his family. He was very close to his older brother. I really liked my brother-in-law, and normally I didn't resent the time they spent together, but today was a rough milestone for me and I didn't want to be on my own.

After several failed attempts to reach my closest friends, Donna and Sherry, I pondered what to do with my time alone. It was a scorching August day, so I assumed they must have gone swimming with their families at one of the local parks. *I bet their husbands are spending the day with them*, I thought grudgingly.

AT HEART

I rolled my long red hair into a barrette at the back of my head and pulled one of Cameron's baseball caps over the top. After coating myself with suntan lotion, I donned my sunglasses and grabbed the keys from the counter before heading out.

I turned my white Honda Civic east onto the Trans-Canada Highway and adjusted the radio station to 98.7 FM, Gander's local station. Singing to the rock 'n' roll oldies helped improve my mood. As I had often done in the past, I found myself turning at the Silent Witnesses Memorial, just a few minutes from town.

Dust billowed around the car as I drove down the steep gravel road leading to the monument. This was a sacred place . . . a place where people died tragically on December 14, 1985. This was the site of the 101st Arrow Air crash when 248 soldiers, known as the Screaming Eagles, and eight crew members perished on the DC-8 when it exploded just after takeoff. No witnesses survived, and to this day the cause of the incident remains a mystery.

My mind flashed back to that tragic day once again. There had been a strained silence in the lobby of the James Paton Memorial Hospital, as each of our triage teams awaited the arrival of casualties. Our disaster plan had been put into action, so that we would receive the wounded and the bodies of the deceased would go to the Canadian Forces Base. I remember how horrified I felt when it was announced that our services were not required because there were no survivors.

I pulled to the side of the road, next to the site's walkway, stepped out of the car into the late afternoon sun, and bypassed the steps leading to the monument. Instead, I strolled farther down, to the base of the Cross of Sacrifice, to kneel and say a prayer for the dead soldiers and crew. It always tore at my heart to think how these soldiers died after returning from the Sinai Desert on a peacekeeping mission. Such a waste of honourable souls.

When I finished praying, I stood and looked at the inscription, which extended vertically beneath the cross. It read, "Rendezvous With Destiny," the motto of the 101st Airborne. Sad to think their fate would be to die here, so tragically, and so far from home.

I ascended the steep rocky walkway to the crash site. At the monument, I passed by a woman about my age who was reading the list of victims' names. She was short-statured with dark hair that fell in waves around her shoulders. I thought she must be a tourist because she wore a jacket and slacks on this hot day, with a camera case looped over her shoulder.

I continued my trek to the statue of a soldier who held the hand of a boy to his right and a girl to his left. I brushed the tendrils of the girl's hair as I often did on visits, and a lump formed in my throat again to see the olive branches held by the children as a symbol of peace.

I dismounted the large rock I was standing on next to the statue and, as I walked by the woman at the monument, I heard sobs coming from her.

"Are you okay?" I asked, and handed her a tissue.

She nodded. "This place is so beautiful and so sad at the same time."

"Yes, it is. I've wept many tears here myself," I replied. Extending my hand, I said, "My name is Sandy."

Shaking my hand, she said, "I'm Miriam. My fiancé was one of the soldiers who died here, and today would have been his birthday. I've always wanted to visit the place where Johnny died, but I couldn't afford the airfare until now."

"I'm so sorry for your loss," I choked out. "Today is my birthday also. I was feeling a little down about turning forty, but I guess I should feel lucky to be alive to celebrate it."

"Yes, there are worse fates than turning forty. I wish Johnny could have turned forty."

Even after twenty years, the pain of loss was vividly obvious in Miriam's troubled eyes. I suddenly felt very thankful for having Cameron in my life and didn't know what I would do if anything ever happened to him. He was just a few miles away, playing golf, and I was no longer upset with him.

Over the course of the day, Miriam disclosed some of her memories of Johnny and the life they had shared, along with their hopes and dreams for the future. They had been high school sweethearts and planned to marry when Johnny's military training was completed. But he was called to active duty in the Middle East, so they postponed their wedding. He promised they would be married as soon as he returned.

She talked of the last time she saw him as he kissed her

goodbye. They were on the front veranda of her parents' home in Oak Grove, Kentucky before he left for his tour of duty. She had wept openly, and there were tears in his eyes as well when he turned away from her for the last time. She thought their separation would be lengthy, but she never imagined it would be for a lifetime.

Miriam had finished sealing the last of the wedding invitations when she received the devastating news that her beloved Johnny would not be returning. *It must certainly be some sort of mistake . . . Johnny had completed his duty and survived war. How could he have died on his way back home, especially in a safe place like Newfoundland?*

The Silent Witnesses Memorial had always been a sad and sacred place for me, but it was a place of heartache for those who had lost loved ones there. Only now did I realize how much.

It was late in the evening when I said goodbye to Miriam. Time had slipped away from us as we sat on the top clearing, surrounded by seven small American flags where the plane had first made impact with the earth. The view was breathtaking as we looked down from our perch toward the statue, the cross, and the beautifully serene Gander Lake below. If only the trees could talk and tell us what really happened here on that cold December day in 1985. What secrets would they reveal about the incident? What would they tell us about the 256 witnesses who will forever keep their silence? We'll never know, but at least the passage of time has changed this area of tragedy to one of tranquility and remembrance.

When I returned home, there was a message on my answering machine from Donna. She asked me to join her for an iced tea by the pool. I scribbled a quick note to let Cameron know where I was in case he returned early, although I didn't think there was much chance of that. When he was playing golf with his brother, it usually ended with a few drinks at the Golf Club afterwards. I probably wouldn't see him for the night.

Donna's house was just four doors down on the other side of the street, so I slipped on my sandals and strolled down the road. When I opened the gate to her backyard, a throng of voices bellowed, "Surprise!"

For a second I didn't know what was happening, until I focused on Cameron at the head of the group, surrounded by the smiling faces of my friends and family. They had successfully pulled off a surprise party for me!

Cameron hugged me and said, "Are you still mad at me?"

"Of course not," I said. "I'm just thankful you're alive."

He look puzzled by my statement. Then he grinned. "Is it okay if I play golf tomorrow?"

Angela's Wings

ROBERT HUNT

The hawk dipped and turned his wings perpendicular to the ground as he changed direction and swooped off toward his prey. He turned his wings on an angle, adjusting his course, then dived. The tiny field mouse never saw him, and scurried along its path to a small copse of trees. When his prey was just a few feet and only seconds from its goal, the hawk veered and came in directly behind the unsuspecting field mouse. With deadly precision, he swooped in and grasped the tiny animal in his razor-sharp talons. The mouse struggled valiantly, but it was all in vain. Its fate was sealed, and it would run no more.

Angela was eleven years old when she witnessed this awesome bird hunt his quarry near her home in Deer Lake.

AT HEART

The little girl was amazed at how the hawk had pinpointed the field mouse from high above and in a matter of seconds had claimed it from the ground. Ever since that day, she knew she wanted to fly. To be in balance with nature, as she put it. Angela wanted to be like that hawk, to soar on the wind and make the skies her own. The grace, beauty, and dignity of the hawk stayed with her all through her childhood and into her adult years.

Returning to the present, she boarded the Cessna aircraft with her Argosy Aviation instructor, Darren Sparks.

"Make sure to check your gear and instruments again, Angela," Darren said. "You won't be able to when you're in the air."

"Darren, you know me better than that," Angela replied. "I always double-check everything before I fly."

When all the pre-flight checks were nearly concluded, Darren said, "Angela, I spoke to your husband yesterday, and he told me that December 19 is your birthday. He asked me to give you part of his birthday present early, so I guess I can tell you about it now."

"What is it," she asked excitedly.

"You can do your solo flight two months earlier than expected. In your training, you have shown me how capable you are of taking an aircraft up alone, so Friday morning she's all yours."

Angela screamed with delight and nearly toppled him over with a fierce hug. She couldn't believe it! Finally, after two years of training, her own solo flight! The hawk and mouse she so often thought about crossed her mind. Her spirit rejoiced as she and Darren flew one last time together in the Cessna, high above Deer Lake and the cares and turmoil of the earth below. She wanted to stay in the air forever. Darren brought Angela back to reality when he told her that her flying time was up and the aircraft was ready to land. She gracefully guided the Cessna through the clouds and made a 180-degree turn before coming in for landing.

When she arrived home, she burst into the house and flung her arms around her husband's neck. She exclaimed, "Cyril, I love you! Thanks so much for talking to Darren about my solo flight."

"You're welcome, honey, but I'm not sure it was a wise decision. Are you sure you're ready to fly alone?"

"Oh, honey, you know better than anyone how hard I've trained. It will be a piece of cake for me! I've got to call Mom. Love you," she said as she raced to the phone.

On Thursday, Angela dropped by the airport hangar to see which craft she would be flying the next day. Darren always surprised his students before their solo flights by taking them into the hangar and picking out which aircraft they were to fly that special day. Darren took her by the arm, asked her to close her eyes, and walked her to the end of the hangar to a curtained-off space. When the partition opened, Angela stood staring at the most beautiful aircraft she had ever seen in her life. She looked at Darren flabbergasted.

"Angela, I have been an instructor for seventeen years and have never seen a student more capable of flying an aircraft than you. So, I had this beauty flown in last night from our main flight school in St. John's. I only allow certain students to take this Cherokee in the air solo, and you are one of them."

Angela looked at the Cherokee PA28-140 as if it were a Greek god. It was a cool black, with silver-black wings. Its metallic paint glowed under the lights in the hangar. So elegant. So regal. The call numbers on the back tail section read 1104. She walked around the side and noticed the name written on its side. *The Hawk* was painted on its tail section in bold white letters. *Aptly named*, she thought.

"She's absolutely beautiful, Darren. So very beautiful! I'll make you proud of me tomorrow, I promise. I won't let you down."

Darren smiled. "I know you won't."

Angela found it difficult to sleep that night. Visions of the *Hawk* slicing through the air while she was at the controls filled her dreams. This is what she had wanted to do ever since she saw the hawk chase the field mouse that day many years ago. Tomorrow she would fulfill her dreams.

Angela was up bright and early to arrive ahead of time for her solo flight. Driving to the airport, she reviewed the pre-flight checks in her mind. She entered the hangar and climbed up the short steps that led into the aircraft. All seemed in order, and when the pre-flight check was complete, she signalled to Darren that everything was okay. She got out of the aircraft and hugged Cyril, staring back at the *Hawk* in all its splendour. *Today, after all these years, you're mine,* Angela thought. She patted the *Hawk*'s insignia on the tail end, walked to the boarding ladder, and stepped into the cockpit.

"Okay, Angela, everything seems fine," Darren shouted over the startup's roar. "Your checks are done and all systems are A-okay. The plane is full and ready for takeoff. Don't forget your final checks when you're ready to taxi to the runway . . . and remember, be careful up there."

"I will, Darren, and thanks for everything," Angela replied, fighting back tears as her instructor and friend gave a thumbs-up.

She looked out through the open hangar and could tell the temperature was below zero, but at least there was no rain or drizzle. Taking a deep breath, she let off on the *Hawk*'s throttle and slowly edged her way out to the ramp. She stopped short of the taxiway Bravo and contacted Control Tower for clearance to take off. A moment later, the tower gave her the weather report, a temperature reading, altimeter check, and clearance to approach the runway. Angela made the last of her instrument checks and proceeded to Runway 02-20 from Taxi Bravo. *This is it,* Angela thought, *just you and me, baby, just you and me.*

"Ground, Cherokee 1104 at Bravo. Permission to proceed to 02-20 for clearance for takeoff."

"Cherokee 1104, Ground. Permission granted for take-off. Proceed Bravo, taxi to 02-20. Await instructions for takeoff."

Angela eased the aircraft ahead and proceeded to take up her position on 02. She waited on the runway for the final call from Ground. Within a few minutes, she was heading down 02 in full takeoff mode. She sped the aircraft down the runway for a thousand feet and pulled the nose up. The *Hawk* pointed upward into the air and toward total freedom. Immediately, Angela felt a surge of adrenaline through her body, feeling like a bird that has just taken flight.

Up the *Hawk* flew until it reached the tower's directive of four thousand feet. Angela checked all systems and levelled out into a perfect glide. She felt as if she had died and gone to heaven! *There is no place like this on earth*, she thought, slipping between grey-white clouds. She dipped her wings in angles and was seduced by the carefree feeling that flying gave her. Up, up into the mighty blue she soared, dipping her wings now and then, becoming seduced by her newfound freedom. She pushed the *Hawk*'s massive weight against wind shear and air pockets as if it were indeed alive and gasping for breath.

Angela dropped the aircraft back toward the earth until it was at an altitude of thirty-six hundred feet. The young pilot turned and sank again to twenty-seven hundred feet, and she was just beginning to level off when she heard a small pop. She continued on, thinking nothing of it, until she heard it again. It sounded like water being forced through a narrow pipe.

The noise turned into a dim rattle, and grew louder still as the aircraft banked to one side. Angela had to veer left to compensate and maintain control while the *Hawk* hit a wind shear. All of a sudden, the noise stopped. In fact, for a split second all noise stopped. Then the engine shuddered, as though awakening from a deep sleep, but it emitted only a cough and a sputter. Angela checked her instruments and noticed that the carburetor gauge had practically dropped to zero. She understood that the carburetor had possibly iced up from the sub-zero temperatures the *Hawk* encountered while at four thousand feet.

Angela kept calm and thought of her training. *Whatever you do, don't panic* was the first thing that came to her mind. She tried to restart the engine, but to no avail. She tried again, but the second time she knew it was pointless. She radioed Control Tower that she was experiencing problems. Control advised her to drop down to twelve hundred feet and level off.

Trying hard not to panic now, Angela checked her wind readings and dropped another hundred feet into an air pocket. Staying calm was her main objective now. She now had gliding control over the aircraft and looked ahead in search of the nearest runway.

"Ground, this is Cherokee 1104. By the look of my gauges, I think I am experiencing engine coolant freeze-up, maybe because of the altitude. I have tried to restart my engine twice, but with no luck. I will drop to one thousand feet and retry. If I still have no luck, I will try to find a wind pocket and glide her in. Over."

"Cherokee 1104. Read you loud and clear. Permission granted to drop to one thousand feet. Please advise when you do so. I will notify all emergency vehicles to stand by."

"Roger, Ground. Will advise you when I drop to one thousand feet. Over and out."

While Angela was communicating with the tower, she had turned her head and glanced out toward the open sky. Something had caught her attention. Now she could see it for what it was. There, flying parallel to the Cherokee, was a beautiful, black, silver-streaked hawk! *This is impossible*, she thought. But the hawk, as if in answer to her thoughts, turned slightly away from her, as if to say *follow me*. She gripped the wheel, gave it a slight nudge, and headed toward the hawk. The small plane responded and fell in directly behind the bird. The wind took hold of the aircraft, and Angela felt a small thump, as if God Himself was holding the aircraft in His Hands. The hawk stayed at a slight downward angle, dropping evenly through the clouds.

The Cherokee followed, in sync with the majestic bird. It seemed as though they were one. The plane then dropped through an opening in the clouds, and a short distance ahead Angela could see the airport runway.

"Ground, now have maintained altitude of one thousand feet. Will try to drop lower to see if engine will start."

"Roger that, Cherokee 1104. Please advise when you do so. And good luck."

Angela spun the aircraft into a twenty-degree roll, performing a wing-to-wing pattern so she could attract attention on the ground. She dropped lower and levelled at six hundred feet. Uttering a silent prayer, she turned the key to the engine once more, and suddenly, miraculously, it sprang to life! Her heart raced as she again took control of the aircraft.

"Ground, this is Cherokee 1104. I now have dropped from one thousand feet to six hundred feet. Also, I am now in full control of this aircraft. Have Runway 29 in plain view. Permission to land."

"Cherokee 1104. Glad to see you have control of your aircraft back. Permission granted to land on Runway 29. Emergency crew will be standing by. I was watching you manoeuvre that aircraft, 1104; it was a great bit of flying."

Angela held the aircraft level as she turned in for her final approach. She looked around for the hawk, but he was nowhere to be seen. She came in on the runway, levelled off, and brought the plane down smoothly. Blowing out a sigh of relief, she taxied toward the hangar. Suddenly, the hawk appeared next to the Cherokee, flying close to the wing. He then changed direction, turning as if to say goodbye to the young pilot.

"Thanks, old friend," Angela said with a lump in her throat. "If not for you and your guidance up there, I might not be alive. I will never forget you"

The hawk flew off into the clear, blue sky, until it became little more than a speck in the distance, and then was gone, leaving the young pilot alone with her special plane.

Acknowledgements

A special thank you to Dr. Tom Cantwell, Dr. Stephanie van Wyk, Dr. Jaco Maritz, and Dr. Joseph Tumilty for consultation in your areas of medical expertise. Thanks to Don Kelly for direction regarding forestry issues.

We would like to acknowledge Cal Smith and Marilyn Anthony for proofreading and feedback on the manuscript before submission. In addition, thank you to Allison Fox, Steve White, and Mike Kelly for taking the time to read these stories.

Heartfelt appreciation to all the readers, both acquaintances and strangers, who have contacted us to ask when we would be publishing our second book. The positive response to our first publication, *Christmas Memories*, has been overwhelming and certainly exceeded our expectations.

Lisa extends a personal note of thanks to Mike, for the gift of the hand-held transcriber. It was an invaluable asset in the writing of this book. Robert would like to thank many of his co-workers at the St. John's International Airport.

About the Authors

LISA IVANY lives in Gander and works as a psychiatric secretary during the daytime, and as an orthopaedic executive assistant at night. In her spare time she writes short stories and poetry, the latter of which has won a Golden Poet's Award. Lisa is co-author of *Christmas Memories: Stories of Newfoundland and Labrador* and has published three feature articles and several poems.

ROBERT HUNT resides in St. John's and works at the St. John's International Airport. He is co-author of the bestselling *Christmas Memories*. On his retirement from the airport, he plans to pursue his writing career on a full-time basis.